Hans Holbein, Henry N. Humphreys

Hans Holbein's Celebrated Dance of Death

Illustrated by a Series of Photo-Lithographic Facsimiles from the Copy of the First

Edition Now in the British Museum. Accompanied by Explanatory Descriptions and

a Concise History of the Origin and Subseque

Hans Holbein, Henry N. Humphreys

Hans Holbein's Celebrated Dance of Death
Illustrated by a Series of Photo-Lithographic Facsimiles from the Copy of the First Edition Now in the British Museum. Accompanied by Explanatory Descriptions and a Concise History of the Origin and Subseque

ISBN/EAN: 9783337394127

Printed in Europe, USA, Canada, Australia, Japan

Cover: Foto ©Andreas Hilbeck / pixelio.de

More available books at **www.hansebooks.com**

entitled "Van drén Konygen," and "Van den doden Konigen, und van den levenden Konigen." There were also English versions of the legend, one of which is preserved among the Arundel manuscripts in the British Museum. This English version of the "Three Living and the Three Dead," in addition to the interest of the subject, is remarkable as affording a curious example of the English language in a transition state. For instance, in the rude illumination at the beginning three kings, who are represented as pursuing the exciting amusement of the chase in a pleasant wood, suddenly meet three skeletons, at the sight of which, being naturally struck with dismay, the first king is represented as saying,—

> Ich am afert, lo what ich se
> Me thinketh hit beth develes thre;

to which the first skeleton replies,—

> Ich wes wel fair—such skelton be—
> For Godes love be wer by me;

which, put into rather more modern form, would read,—

> I am afeard !—lo ! what d'I see?
> Methinks that it be devils three;

the response being,—

> I, once well fair, now skel(e)ton be;
> For God's love, then, be warned by me.

The characters of this legend are often changed in the different versions; sometimes they are a king, a queen, and a nobleman; sometimes three noble youths in gaily-broidered suits, and bearing richly-adorned weapons, revelling, as hunters, in the luxuries and privileges of rank and wealth. There is a very early representation of this version of the "Three Living and the Three Dead" in the church at Brie, near Metz.

Orcagna's celebrated "Triumph of Death" in the Campo Santo, at Pisa, painted in the 14th century, may be called an Italianized version of this legend. The three principal figures are the three kings of the original legend, but they are accompanied by their mistresses, and St. Macarius himself takes the place of the three skeletons, showing to the living kings three open graves, in which lie the bodies of three dead kings. In another part of the composition Death is symbolized by a female figure furnished with bats' wings and claws, and bearing a scythe, with which she sweeps down popes, emperors, kings, and others of all classes.

Here, then, we already find an extension of the range of the legend of St. Macarius to all classes, as carried out more definitely and distinctly in the "Dance of Death," which no doubt owed much of its immediate and lasting popularity, as previously suggested, to its fearless carrying out, in a more modern and expressive form, of the well-known verses of Horace—

> Pallida mors æquo pulsat pede pauperum tabernas,
> Regumque turres.

The more Northern expansion of this subject, whether we consider it as a series of stanzas forming a poem entitled "The Dance of Death," or as

a mere extension of the legend of St. Macarius, or as an original and more extensive work of analogous character, to which new verses were added from time to time as fresh characters were introduced, is asserted to have been of German origin,—a conclusion arrived at from the fact that the French and Latin verses attached to the earliest printed editions of the " Dance of Death " are stated, in more than one of the short prefaces or titles attached to those works, to have been translated from the German. On the other hand, with a view to explain the meaning of the term " Macabre," under which the first editions of the " Dance of Death " were issued in France, a few observations of an apparently opposite tendency may be conveniently made in this place. Firstly, if a German author either extended the poem of St. Macarius, or composed another of analogous but more extensive character, it seems probable that he would, or might, have founded his title on the name of the original author, and have termed his work the Macarian or Machabrian Dance, as some writers on the subject have suggested; and an allusion closely bordering upon that suggestion occurs in the celebrated La Vallière catalogue, in which a MS. " Dance of Death " is described, with the note, " On l'a dit composé par un nommé Macabre." That the spirit of German satire of the period did actually run in that direction, both poetically and pictorially, is proved by the works of Sebastian Brandt, whose " Ship of Fools," in which personifications of all the leading types of human folly are represented as embarked in the Ship of Life, is an allegory closely resembling, in many respects, the " Dance of Death," while its profuse illustrations are not very dissimilar in general spirit to those belonging to that subject. It is worthy of note, also, that the " Ship of Fools " was translated from the German into French as " La Nef des Fous," and was soon followed by a companion work devoted exclusively to women, under the title of " La Nef des Folles," just as the first edition of the " Dance of Death," which was printed in France under the name of " La Danse Macabre," was as immediately followed by " La Danse Macabre des Femmes." Nevertheless, it does not appear probable that the term Macabre originated in Germany. The supposition that the name of the German poet was Macabre is, indeed, far less probable than that he might have named the poem after St. Macarius, while neither hypothesis is borne out by the known facts of the case, for we do not find a single German version bearing the title of " Macabre," or " Macabrean," but simply that of the " Doden Dänze," or " Todten Taenze." Was it, then, a French author who composed the poem? and, if so, was the title founded upon the name of St. Macarius, or derived from some other source? Van Prael suggested that Magbar and Magbarah* were Arabic names for a cemetery; and this is possibly a hint that may eventually lead to a more satisfactory explanation of the term than that founded on the name of St. Macarius, and there is collateral evidence of some weight that may be brought forward in support of this view. It is well known that Nicholas Flamel, who lived in the last half of the 14th century, and who enjoyed the various reputation of author, merchant, alchemist, and astrologer, was also a munificent benefactor of

* The Bibliophile Jacob ridicules this derivation, and jocosely suggests in its stead *Abracadabra.*

entitled "Van drén Konygen," and "Van den doden Konigen, und van
den levenden Konigen." There were also English versions of the legend,
one of which is preserved among the Arundel manuscripts in the British
Museum. This English version of the "Three Living and the Three
Dead," in addition to the interest of the subject, is remarkable as affording
a curious example of the English language in a transition state. For
instance, in the rude illumination at the beginning three kings, who are
represented as pursuing the exciting amusement of the chase in a pleasant
wood, suddenly meet three skeletons, at the sight of which, being naturally
struck with dismay, the first king is represented as saying,—

> Ich am afert, lo what ich se
> Me thinketh hit beth develes thre ;

to which the first skeleton replies,—

> Ich wes wel fair—such skelton be—
> For Godes love be wer by me ;

which, put into rather more modern form, would read,—

> I am afeard !—lo ! what d'I see?
> Methinks that it be devils three ;

the response being,—

> I, once well fair, now skel(e)ton be ;
> For God's love, then, be warned by me.

The characters of this legend are often changed in the different versions ;
sometimes they are a king, a queen, and a nobleman ; sometimes three
noble youths in gaily-broidered suits, and bearing richly-adorned weapons,
revelling, as hunters, in the luxuries and privileges of rank and wealth.
There is a very early representation of this version of the "Three Living
and the Three Dead " in the church at Brie, near Metz.

Orcagna's celebrated "Triumph of Death " in the Campo Santo, at Pisa,
painted in the 14th century, may be called an Italianized version of this
legend. The three principal figures are the three kings of the original legend,
but they are accompanied by their mistresses, and St. Macarius himself
takes the place of the three skeletons, showing to the living kings three open
graves, in which lie the bodies of three dead kings. In another part of the
composition Death is symbolized by a female figure furnished with bats'
wings and claws, and bearing a scythe, with which she sweeps down popes,
emperors, kings, and others of all classes.

Here, then, we already find an extension of the range of the legend of
St. Macarius to all classes, as carried out more definitely and distinctly
in the "Dance of Death," which no doubt owed much of its immediate
and lasting popularity, as previously suggested, to its fearless carrying out,
in a more modern and expressive form, of the well-known verses of Horace—

> Pallida mors æquo pulsat pede pauperum tabernas,
> Regumque turres.

The more Northern expansion of this subject, whether we consider it as
a series of stanzas forming a poem entitled "The Dance of Death," or as

a mere extension of the legend of St. Macarius, or as an original and more extensive work of analogous character, to which new verses were added from time to time as fresh characters were introduced, is asserted to have been of German origin,—a conclusion arrived at from the fact that the French and Latin verses attached to the earliest printed editions of the " Dance of Death " are stated, in more than one of the short prefaces or titles attached to those works, to have been translated from the German. On the other hand, with a view to explain the meaning of the term "Macabre," under which the first editions of the " Dance of Death " were issued in France, a few observations of an apparently opposite tendency may be conveniently made in this place. Firstly, if a German author either extended the poem of St. Macarius, or composed another of analogous but more extensive character, it seems probable that he would, or might, have founded his title on the name of the original author, and have termed his work the Macarian or Machabrian Dance, as some writers on the subject have suggested; and an allusion closely bordering upon that suggestion occurs in the celebrated La Vallière catalogue, in which a MS. " Dance of Death " is described, with the note, " On l'a dit composé par un nommé Macabre." That the spirit of German satire of the period did actually run in that direction, both poetically and pictorially, is proved by the works of Sebastian Brandt, whose " Ship of Fools," in which personifications of all the leading types of human folly are represented as embarked in the Ship of Life, is an allegory closely resembling, in many respects, the " Dance of Death," while its profuse illustrations are not very dissimilar in general spirit to those belonging to that subject. It is worthy of note, also, that the " Ship of Fools " was translated from the German into French as "La Nef des Fous," and was soon followed by a companion work devoted exclusively to women, under the title of " La Nef des Folles," just as the first edition of the " Dance of Death," which was printed in France under the name of "La Danse Macabre," was as immediately followed by "La Danse Macabre des Femmes." Nevertheless, it does not appear probable that the term Macabre originated in Germany. The supposition that the name of the German poet was Macabre is, indeed, far less probable than that he might have named the poem after St. Macarius, while neither hypothesis is borne out by the known facts of the case, for we do not find a single German version bearing the title of " Macabre," or " Macabrean," but simply that of the " Doden Dänze," or "Todten Taenze." Was it, then, a French author who composed the poem? and, if so, was the title founded upon the name of St. Macarius, or derived from some other source? Van Prael suggested that Magbar and Magbarah* were Arabic names for a cemetery; and this is possibly a hint that may eventually lead to a more satisfactory explanation of the term than that founded on the name of St. Macarius, and there is collateral evidence of some weight that may be brought forward in support of this view. It is well known that Nicholas Flamel, who lived in the last half of the 14th century, and who enjoyed the various reputation of author, merchant, alchemist, and astrologer, was also a munificent benefactor of

* The Bibliophile Jacob ridicules this derivation, and jocosely suggests in its stead *Abracadabra.*

entitled "Van drén Konygen," and "Van den doden Konigen, und van den levenden Konigen." There were also English versions of the legend, one of which is preserved among the Arundel manuscripts in the British Museum. This English version of the "Three Living and the Three Dead," in addition to the interest of the subject, is remarkable as affording a curious example of the English language in a transition state. For instance, in the rude illumination at the beginning three kings, who are represented as pursuing the exciting amusement of the chase in a pleasant wood, suddenly meet three skeletons, at the sight of which, being naturally struck with dismay, the first king is represented as saying,—

> Ich am afert, lo what ich se
> Me thinketh hit beth develes thre ;

to which the first skeleton replies,—

> Ich wes wel fair—such skelton be—
> For Godes love be wer by me ;

which, put into rather more modern form, would read,—

> I am afeard !—lo ! what d'I see ?
> Methinks that it be devils three ;

the response being,—

> I, once well fair, now skel(e)ton be ;
> For God's love, then, be warned by me.

The characters of this legend are often changed in the different versions ; sometimes they are a king, a queen, and a nobleman ; sometimes three noble youths in gaily-broidered suits, and bearing richly-adorned weapons, revelling, as hunters, in the luxuries and privileges of rank and wealth. There is a very early representation of this version of the "Three Living and the Three Dead" in the church at Brie, near Metz.

Orcagna's celebrated "Triumph of Death" in the Campo Santo, at Pisa, painted in the 14th century, may be called an Italianized version of this legend. The three principal figures are the three kings of the original legend, but they are accompanied by their mistresses, and St. Macarius himself takes the place of the three skeletons, showing to the living kings three open graves, in which lie the bodies of three dead kings. In another part of the composition Death is symbolized by a female figure furnished with bats' wings and claws, and bearing a scythe, with which she sweeps down popes, emperors, kings, and others of all classes.

Here, then, we already find an extension of the range of the legend of St. Macarius to all classes, as carried out more definitely and distinctly in the "Dance of Death," which no doubt owed much of its immediate and lasting popularity, as previously suggested, to its fearless carrying out, in a more modern and expressive form, of the well-known verses of Horace—

> Pallida mors æquo pulsat pede pauperum tabernas,
>   Regumque turres.

The more Northern expansion of this subject, whether we consider it as a series of stanzas forming a poem entitled "The Dance of Death," or as

a mere extension of the legend of St. Macarius, or as an original and more extensive work of analogous character, to which new verses were added from time to time as fresh characters were introduced, is asserted to have been of German origin,—a conclusion arrived at from the fact that the French and Latin verses attached to the earliest printed editions of the "Dance of Death" are stated, in more than one of the short prefaces or titles attached to those works, to have been translated from the German. On the other hand, with a view to explain the meaning of the term "Macabre," under which the first editions of the "Dance of Death" were issued in France, a few observations of an apparently opposite tendency may be conveniently made in this place. Firstly, if a German author either extended the poem of St. Macarius, or composed another of analogous but more extensive character, it seems probable that he would, or might, have founded his title on the name of the original author, and have termed his work the Macarian or Machabrian Dance, as some writers on the subject have suggested; and an allusion closely bordering upon that suggestion occurs in the celebrated La Vallière catalogue, in which a MS. "Dance of Death" is described, with the note, "On l'a dit composé par un nommé Macabre." That the spirit of German satire of the period did actually run in that direction, both poetically and pictorially, is proved by the works of Sebastian Brandt, whose "Ship of Fools," in which personifications of all the leading types of human folly are represented as embarked in the Ship of Life, is an allegory closely resembling, in many respects, the "Dance of Death," while its profuse illustrations are not very dissimilar in general spirit to those belonging to that subject. It is worthy of note, also, that the "Ship of Fools" was translated from the German into French as "La Nef des Fous," and was soon followed by a. companion work devoted exclusively to women, under the title of "La Nef des Folles," just as the first edition of the "Dance of Death," which was printed in France under the name of "La Danse Macabre," was as immediately followed by "La Danse Macabre des Femmes." Nevertheless, it does not appear probable that the term Macabre originated in Germany. The supposition that the name of the German poet was Macabre is, indeed, far less probable than that he might have named the poem after St. Macarius, while neither hypothesis is borne out by the known facts of the case, for we do not find a single German version bearing the title of "Macabre," or "Macabrean," but simply that of the "Doden Dänze," or "Todten Taenze." Was it, then, a French author who composed the poem? and, if so, was the title founded upon the name of St. Macarius, or derived from some other source? Van Prael suggested that Magbar and Magbarah* were Arabic names for a cemetery; and this is possibly a hint that may eventually lead to a more satisfactory explanation of the term than that founded on the name of St. Macarius, and there is collateral evidence of some weight that may be brought forward in support of this view. It is well known that Nicholas Flamel, who lived in the last half of the 14th century, and who enjoyed the various reputation of author, merchant, alchemist, and astrologer, was also a munificent benefactor of

---

* The Bibliophile Jacob ridicules this derivation, and jocosely suggests in its stead *Abracadabra.*

entitled "Van drén Konygen," and "Van den doden Konigen, und van den levenden Konigen." There were also English versions of the legend, one of which is preserved among the Arundel manuscripts in the British Museum. This English version of the "Three Living and the Three Dead," in addition to the interest of the subject, is remarkable as affording a curious example of the English language in a transition state. For instance, in the rude illumination at the beginning three kings, who are represented as pursuing the exciting amusement of the chase in a pleasant wood, suddenly meet three skeletons, at the sight of which, being naturally struck with dismay, the first king is represented as saying,—

> Ich am afert, lo what ich se
> Me thinketh hit beth develes thre ;

to which the first skeleton replies,—

> Ich wes wel fair—such skelton be—
> For Godes love be wer by me ;

which, put into rather more modern form, would read,—

> I am afeard !—lo ! what d'I see ?
> Methinks that it be devils three ;

the response being,—

> I, once well fair, now skel(e)ton be ;
> For God's love, then, be warned by me.

The characters of this legend are often changed in the different versions ; sometimes they are a king, a queen, and a nobleman ; sometimes three noble youths in gaily-broidered suits, and bearing richly-adorned weapons, revelling, as hunters, in the luxuries and privileges of rank and wealth. There is a very early representation of this version of the "Three Living and the Three Dead" in the church at Brie, near Metz.

Orcagna's celebrated "Triumph of Death" in the Campo Santo, at Pisa, painted in the 14th century, may be called an Italianized version of this legend. The three principal figures are the three kings of the original legend, but they are accompanied by their mistresses, and St. Macarius himself takes the place of the three skeletons, showing to the living kings three open graves, in which lie the bodies of three dead kings. In another part of the composition Death is symbolized by a female figure furnished with bats' wings and claws, and bearing a scythe, with which she sweeps down popes, emperors, kings, and others of all classes.

Here, then, we already find an extension of the range of the legend of St. Macarius to all classes, as carried out more definitely and distinctly in the "Dance of Death," which no doubt owed much of its immediate and lasting popularity, as previously suggested, to its fearless carrying out, in a more modern and expressive form, of the well-known verses of Horace—

> Pallida mors æquo pulsat pede pauperum tabernas,
> Regumque turres.

The more Northern expansion of this subject, whether we consider it as a series of stanzas forming a poem entitled "The Dance of Death," or as

a mere extension of the legend of St. Macarius, or as an original and more extensive work of analogous character, to which new verses were added from time to time as fresh characters were introduced, is asserted to have been of German origin,—a conclusion arrived at from the fact that the French and Latin verses attached to the earliest printed editions of the " Dance of Death " are stated, in more than one of the short prefaces or titles attached to those works, to have been translated from the German. On the other hand, with a view to explain the meaning of the term " Macabre," under which the first editions of the " Dance of Death " were issued in France, a few observations of an apparently opposite tendency may be conveniently made in this place. Firstly, if a German author either extended the poem of St. Macarius, or composed another of analogous but more extensive character, it seems probable that he would, or might, have founded his title on the name of the original author, and have termed his work the Macarian or Machabrian Dance, as some writers on the subject have suggested; and an allusion closely bordering upon that suggestion occurs in the celebrated La Vallière catalogue, in which a MS. " Dance of Death " is described, with the note, " On l'a dit composé par un nommé Macabre." That the spirit of German satire of the period did actually run in that direction, both poetically and pictorially, is proved by the works of Sebastian Brandt, whose " Ship of Fools," in which personifications of all the leading types of human folly are represented as embarked in the Ship of Life, is an allegory closely resembling, in many respects, the " Dance of Death," while its profuse illustrations are not very dissimilar in general spirit to those belonging to that subject. It is worthy of note, also, that the " Ship of Fools " was translated from the German into French as " La Nef des Fous," and was soon followed by a companion work devoted exclusively to women, under the title of " La Nef des Folles," just as the first edition of the " Dance of Death," which was printed in France under the name of " La Danse Macabre," was as immediately followed by " La Danse Macabre des Femmes." Nevertheless, it does not appear probable that the term Macabre originated in Germany. The supposition that the name of the German poet was Macabre is, indeed, far less probable than that he might have named the poem after St. Macarius, while neither hypothesis is borne out by the known facts of the case, for we do not find a single German version bearing the title of " Macabre," or " Macabrean," but simply that of the " Doden Dänze," or " Todten Taenze." Was it, then, a French author who composed the poem? and, if so, was the title founded upon the name of St. Macarius, or derived from some other source? Van Prael suggested that Magbar and Magbarah* were Arabic names for a cemetery; and this is possibly a hint that may eventually lead to a more satisfactory explanation of the term than that founded on the name of St. Macarius, and there is collateral evidence of some weight that may be brought forward in support of this view. It is well known that Nicholas Flamel, who lived in the last half of the 14th century, and who enjoyed the various reputation of author, merchant, alchemist, and astrologer, was also a munificent benefactor of

* The Bibliophile Jacob ridicules this derivation, and jocosely suggests in its stead *Abracadabra*.

entitled "Van drén Konygen," and "Van den doden Konigen, und van den levenden Konigen." There were also English versions of the legend, one of which is preserved among the Arundel manuscripts in the British Museum. This English version of the "Three Living and the Three Dead," in addition to the interest of the subject, is remarkable as affording a curious example of the English language in a transition state. For instance, in the rude illumination at the beginning three kings, who are represented as pursuing the exciting amusement of the chase in a pleasant wood, suddenly meet three skeletons, at the sight of which, being naturally struck with dismay, the first king is represented as saying,—

> Ich am afert, lo what ich se
> Me thinketh hit beth develes thre ;

to which the first skeleton replies,—

> Ich wes wel fair—such skelton be—
> For Godes love be wer by me ;

which, put into rather more modern form, would read,—

> I am afeard !—lo ! what d'I see ?
> Methinks that it be devils three ;

the response being,—

> I, once well fair, now skel(e)ton be ;
> For God's love, then, be warned by me.

The characters of this legend are often changed in the different versions ; sometimes they are a king, a queen, and a nobleman ; sometimes three noble youths in gaily-broidered suits, and bearing richly-adorned weapons, revelling, as hunters, in the luxuries and privileges of rank and wealth. There is a very early representation of this version of the "Three Living and the Three Dead " in the church at Brie, near Metz.

Orcagna's celebrated "Triumph of Death" in the Campo Santo, at Pisa, painted in the 14th century, may be called an Italianized version of this legend. The three principal figures are the three kings of the original legend, but they are accompanied by their mistresses, and St. Macarius himself takes the place of the three skeletons, showing to the living kings three open graves, in which lie the bodies of three dead kings. In another part of the composition Death is symbolized by a female figure furnished with bats' wings and claws, and bearing a scythe, with which she sweeps down popes, emperors, kings, and others of all classes.

Here, then, we already find an extension of the range of the legend of St. Macarius to all classes, as carried out more definitely and distinctly in the "Dance of Death," which no doubt owed much of its immediate and lasting popularity, as previously suggested, to its fearless carrying out, in a more modern and expressive form, of the well-known verses of Horace—

> Pallida mors æquo pulsat pede pauperum tabernas,
> Regumque turres.

The more Northern expansion of this subject, whether we consider it as a series of stanzas forming a poem entitled "The Dance of Death," or as

a mere extension of the legend of St. Macarius, or as an original and more extensive work of analogous character, to which new verses were added from time to time as fresh characters were introduced, is asserted to have been of German origin,—a conclusion arrived at from the fact that the French and Latin verses attached to the earliest printed editions of the " Dance of Death " are stated, in more than one of the short prefaces or titles attached to those works, to have been translated from the German. On the other hand, with a view to explain the meaning of the term "Macabre," under which the first editions of the " Dance of Death" were issued in France, a few observations of an apparently opposite tendency may be conveniently made in this place. Firstly, if a German author either extended the poem of St. Macarius, or composed another of analogous but more extensive character, it seems probable that he would, or might, have founded his title on the name of the original author, and have termed his work the Macarian or Machabrian Dance, as some writers on the subject have suggested; and an allusion closely bordering upon that suggestion occurs in the celebrated La Vallière catalogue, in which a MS. "Dance of Death" is described, with the note, "On l'a dit composé par un nommé Macabre." That the spirit of German satire of the period did actually run in that direction, both poetically and pictorially, is proved by the works of Sebastian Brandt, whose "Ship of Fools," in which personifications of all the leading types of human folly are represented as embarked in the Ship of Life, is an allegory closely resembling, in many respects, the "Dance of Death," while its profuse illustrations are not very dissimilar in general spirit to those belonging to that subject. It is worthy of note, also, that the "Ship of Fools" was translated from the German into French as "La Nef des Fous," and was soon followed by a companion work devoted exclusively to women, under the title of "La Nef des Folles," just as the first edition of the "Dance of Death," which was printed in France under the name of "La Danse Macabre," was as immediately followed by "La Danse Macabre des Femmes." Nevertheless, it does not appear probable that the term Macabre originated in Germany. The supposition that the name of the German poet was Macabre is, indeed, far less probable than that he might have named the poem after St. Macarius, while neither hypothesis is borne out by the known facts of the case, for we do not find a single German version bearing the title of "Macabre," or "Macabrean," but simply that of the "Doden Dänze," or "Todten Taenze." Was it, then, a French author who composed the poem? and, if so, was the title founded upon the name of St. Macarius, or derived from some other source? Van Prael suggested that Magbar and Magbarah* were Arabic names for a cemetery; and this is possibly a hint that may eventually lead to a more satisfactory explanation of the term than that founded on the name of St. Macarius, and there is collateral evidence of some weight that may be brought forward in support of this view. It is well known that Nicholas Flamel, who lived in the last half of the 14th century, and who enjoyed the various reputation of author, merchant, alchemist, and astrologer, was also a munificent benefactor of

* The Bibliophile Jacob ridicules this derivation, and jocosely suggests in its stead *Abracadabra*.

entitled "Van drén Konygen," and "Van den doden Konigen, und van den levenden Konigen." There were also English versions of the legend, one of which is preserved among the Arundel manuscripts in the British Museum. This English version of the "Three Living and the Three Dead," in addition to the interest of the subject, is remarkable as affording a curious example of the English language in a transition state. For instance, in the rude illumination at the beginning three kings, who are represented as pursuing the exciting amusement of the chase in a pleasant wood, suddenly meet three skeletons, at the sight of which, being naturally struck with dismay, the first king is represented as saying,—

> Ich am afert, lo what ich se
> Me thinketh hit beth develes thre ;

to which the first skeleton replies,—

> Ich wes wel fair—such skelton be—
> For Godes love be wer by me ;

which, put into rather more modern form, would read,—

> I am afeard !—lo ! what d'I see ?
> Methinks that it be devils three ;

the response being,—

> I, once well fair, now skel(e)ton be ;
> For God's love, then, be warned by me.

The characters of this legend are often changed in the different versions ; sometimes they are a king, a queen, and a nobleman ; sometimes three noble youths in gaily-broidered suits, and bearing richly-adorned weapons, revelling, as hunters, in the luxuries and privileges of rank and wealth. There is a very early representation of this version of the "Three Living and the Three Dead " in the church at Brie, near Metz.

Orcagna's celebrated "Triumph of Death " in the Campo Santo, at Pisa, painted in the 14th century, may be called an Italianized version of this legend. The three principal figures are the three kings of the original legend, but they are accompanied by their mistresses, and St. Macarius himself takes the place of the three skeletons, showing to the living kings three open graves, in which lie the bodies of three dead kings. In another part of the composition Death is symbolized by a female figure furnished with bats' wings and claws, and bearing a scythe, with which she sweeps down popes, emperors, kings, and others of all classes.

Here, then, we already find an extension of the range of the legend of St. Macarius to all classes, as carried out more definitely and distinctly in the "Dance of Death," which no doubt owed much of its immediate and lasting popularity, as previously suggested, to its fearless carrying out, in a more modern and expressive form, of the well-known verses of Horace—

> Pallida mors æquo pulsat pede pauperum tabernas,
> Regumque turres.

The more Northern expansion of this subject, whether we consider it as a series of stanzas forming a poem entitled "The Dance of Death," or as

a mere extension of the legend of St. Macarius, or as an original and
more extensive work of analogous character, to which new verses were added
from time to time as fresh characters were introduced, is asserted to have
been of German origin,—a conclusion arrived at from the fact that the
French and Latin verses attached to the earliest printed editions of the
" Dance of Death " are stated, in more than one of the short prefaces or
titles attached to those works, to have been translated from the German.
On the other hand, with a view to explain the meaning of the term
" Macabre," under which the first editions of the " Dance of Death " were
issued in France, a few observations of an apparently opposite tendency
may be conveniently made in this place. Firstly, if a German author
either extended the poem of St. Macarius, or composed another of analogous but more extensive character, it seems probable that he would, or
might, have founded his title on the name of the original author, and have
termed his work the Macarian or Machabrian Dance, as some writers
on the subject have suggested ; and an allusion closely bordering upon that
suggestion occurs in the celebrated La Vallière catalogue, in which a
MS. " Dance of Death " is described, with the note, " On l'a dit composé
par un nommé Macabre." That the spirit of German satire of the period
did actually run in that direction, both poetically and pictorially, is proved
by the works of Sebastian Brandt, whose " Ship of Fools," in which personifications of all the leading types of human folly are represented as
embarked in the Ship of Life, is an allegory closely resembling, in many
respects, the " Dance of Death," while its profuse illustrations are not
very dissimilar in general spirit to those belonging to that subject. It is
worthy of note, also, that the " Ship of Fools " was translated from
the German into French as "La Nef des Fous," and was soon followed
by a companion work devoted exclusively to women, under the title of
" La Nef des Folles," just as the first edition of the " Dance of Death,"
which was printed in France under the name of "La Danse Macabre,"
was as immediately followed by " La Danse Macabre des Femmes."
Nevertheless, it does not appear probable that the term Macabre originated
in Germany. The supposition that the name of the German poet was
Macabre is, indeed, far less probable than that he might have named the
poem after St. Macarius, while neither hypothesis is borne out by the
known facts of the case, for we do not find a single German version bearing
the title of " Macabre," or " Macabrean," but simply that of the " Doden
Dänze," or " Todten Taenze." Was it, then, a French author who composed the poem ? and, if so, was the title founded upon the name of
St. Macarius, or derived from some other source ? Van Prael suggested
that Magbar and Magbarah* were Arabic names for a cemetery ; and this is
possibly a hint that may eventually lead to a more satisfactory explanation
of the term than that founded on the name of St. Macarius, and there is
collateral evidence of some weight that may be brought forward in support
of this view. It is well known that Nicholas Flamel, who lived in the last
half of the 14th century, and who enjoyed the various reputation of author,
merchant, alchemist, and astrologer, was also a munificent benefactor of

* The Bibliophile Jacob ridicules this derivation, and jocosely suggests in its stead
Abracadabra.

entitled "Van drén Konygen," and "Van den doden Konigen, und van den levenden Konigen." There were also English versions of the legend, one of which is preserved among the Arundel manuscripts in the British Museum. This English version of the "Three Living and the Three Dead," in addition to the interest of the subject, is remarkable as affording a curious example of the English language in a transition state. For instance, in the rude illumination at the beginning three kings, who are represented as pursuing the exciting amusement of the chase in a pleasant wood, suddenly meet three skeletons, at the sight of which, being naturally struck with dismay, the first king is represented as saying,—

> Ich am afert, lo what ich se
> Me thinketh hit beth develes thre ;

to which the first skeleton replies,—

> Ich wes wel fair—such skelton be—
> For Godes love be wer by me ;

which, put into rather more modern form, would read,—

> I am afeard !—lo ! what d'I see ?
> Methinks that it be devils three ;

the response being,—

> I, once well fair, now skel(e)ton be ;
> For God's love, then, be warned by me.

The characters of this legend are often changed in the different versions ; sometimes they are a king, a queen, and a nobleman ; sometimes three noble youths in gaily-broidered suits, and bearing richly-adorned weapons, revelling, as hunters, in the luxuries and privileges of rank and wealth. There is a very early representation of this version of the "Three Living and the Three Dead" in the church at Brie, near Metz.

Orcagna's celebrated "Triumph of Death" in the Campo Santo, at Pisa, painted in the 14th century, may be called an Italianized version of this legend. The three principal figures are the three kings of the original legend, but they are accompanied by their mistresses, and St. Macarius himself takes the place of the three skeletons, showing to the living kings three open graves, in which lie the bodies of three dead kings. In another part of the composition Death is symbolized by a female figure furnished with bats' wings and claws, and bearing a scythe, with which she sweeps down popes, emperors, kings, and others of all classes.

Here, then, we already find an extension of the range of the legend of St. Macarius to all classes, as carried out more definitely and distinctly in the "Dance of Death," which no doubt owed much of its immediate and lasting popularity, as previously suggested, to its fearless carrying out, in a more modern and expressive form, of the well-known verses of Horace—

> Pallida mors æquo pulsat pede pauperum tabernas,
> Regumque turres.

The more Northern expansion of this subject, whether we consider it as a series of stanzas forming a poem entitled "The Dance of Death," or as

a mere extension of the legend of St. Macarius, or as an original and more extensive work of analogous character, to which new verses were added from time to time as fresh characters were introduced, is asserted to have been of German origin,—a conclusion arrived at from the fact that the French and Latin verses attached to the earliest printed editions of the " Dance of Death " are stated, in more than one of the short prefaces or titles attached to those works, to have been translated from the German. On the other hand, with a view to explain the meaning of the term " Macabre," under which the first editions of the " Dance of Death " were issued in France, a few observations of an apparently opposite tendency may be conveniently made in this place. Firstly, if a German author either extended the poem of St. Macarius, or composed another of analogous but more extensive character, it seems probable that he would, or might, have founded his title on the name of the original author, and have termed his work the Macarian or Machabrian Dance, as some writers on the subject have suggested ; and an allusion closely bordering upon that suggestion occurs in the celebrated La Vallière catalogue, in which a MS. " Dance of Death " is described, with the note, " On l'a dit composé par un nommé Macabre." That the spirit of German satire of the period did actually run in that direction, both poetically and pictorially, is proved by the works of Sebastian Brandt, whose " Ship of Fools," in which personifications of all the leading types of human folly are represented as embarked in the Ship of Life, is an allegory closely resembling, in many respects, the " Dance of Death," while its profuse illustrations are not very dissimilar in general spirit to those belonging to that subject. It is worthy of note, also, that the " Ship of Fools " was translated from the German into French as " La Nef des Fous," and was soon followed by a companion work devoted exclusively to women, under the title of " La Nef des Folles," just as the first edition of the " Dance of Death," which was printed in France under the name of " La Danse Macabre," was as immediately followed by " La Danse Macabre des Femmes." Nevertheless, it does not appear probable that the term Macabre originated in Germany. The supposition that the name of the German poet was Macabre is, indeed, far less probable than that he might have named the poem after St. Macarius, while neither hypothesis is borne out by the known facts of the case, for we do not find a single German version bearing the title of " Macabre," or " Macabrean," but simply that of the " Doden Dänze," or " Todten Taenze." Was it, then, a French author who composed the poem ? and, if so, was the title founded upon the name of St. Macarius, or derived from some other source ? Van Prael suggested that Magbar and Magbarah* were Arabic names for a cemetery; and this is possibly a hint that may eventually lead to a more satisfactory explanation of the term than that founded on the name of St. Macarius, and there is collateral evidence of some weight that may be brought forward in support of this view. It is well known that Nicholas Flamel, who lived in the last half of the 14th century, and who enjoyed the various reputation of author, merchant, alchemist, and astrologer, was also a munificent benefactor of

* The Bibliophile Jacob ridicules this derivation, and jocosely suggests in its stead *Abracadabra.*

entitled "Van drén Konygen," and "Van den doden Konigen, und van den levenden Konigen." There were also English versions of the legend, one of which is preserved among the Arundel manuscripts in the British Museum. This English version of the "Three Living and the Three Dead," in addition to the interest of the subject, is remarkable as affording a curious example of the English language in a transition state. For instance, in the rude illumination at the beginning three kings, who are represented as pursuing the exciting amusement of the chase in a pleasant wood, suddenly meet three skeletons, at the sight of which, being naturally struck with dismay, the first king is represented as saying,—

> Ich am afert, lo what ich se
> Me thinketh hit beth develes thre ;

to which the first skeleton replies,—

> Ich wes wel fair—such skelton be—
> For Godes love be wer by me ;

which, put into rather more modern form, would read,—

> I am afeard !—lo ! what d'I see ?
> Methinks that it be devils three ;

the response being,—

> I, once well fair, now skel(e)ton be ;
> For God's love, then, be warned by me.

The characters of this legend are often changed in the different versions ; sometimes they are a king, a queen, and a nobleman ; sometimes three noble youths in gaily-broidered suits, and bearing richly-adorned weapons, revelling, as hunters, in the luxuries and privileges of rank and wealth. There is a very early representation of this version of the "Three Living and the Three Dead " in the church at Brie, near Metz.

Orcagna's celebrated " Triumph of Death " in the Campo Santo, at Pisa, painted in the 14th century, may be called an Italianized version of this legend. The three principal figures are the three kings of the original legend, but they are accompanied by their mistresses, and St. Macarius himself takes the place of the three skeletons, showing to the living kings three open graves, in which lie the bodies of three dead kings.   In another part of the composition Death is symbolized by a female figure furnished with bats' wings and claws, and bearing a scythe, with which she sweeps down popes, emperors, kings, and others of all classes.

Here, then, we already find an extension of the range of the legend of St. Macarius to all classes, as carried out more definitely and distinctly in the "Dance of Death," which no doubt owed much of its immediate and lasting popularity, as previously suggested, to its fearless carrying out, in a more modern and expressive form, of the well-known verses of Horace—

> Pallida mors æquo pulsat pede pauperum tabernas,
> Regumque turres.

The more Northern expansion of this subject, whether we consider it as a series of stanzas forming a poem entitled " The Dance of Death," or as

a mere extension of the legend of St. Macarius, or as an original and more extensive work of analogous character, to which new verses were added from time to time as fresh characters were introduced, is asserted to have been of German origin,—a conclusion arrived at from the fact that the French and Latin verses attached to the earliest printed editions of the "Dance of Death" are stated, in more than one of the short prefaces or titles attached to those works, to have been translated from the German. On the other hand, with a view to explain the meaning of the term "Macabre," under which the first editions of the "Dance of Death" were issued in France, a few observations of an apparently opposite tendency may be conveniently made in this place. Firstly, if a German author either extended the poem of St. Macarius, or composed another of analogous but more extensive character, it seems probable that he would, or might, have founded his title on the name of the original author, and have termed his work the Macarian or Machabrian Dance, as some writers on the subject have suggested; and an allusion closely bordering upon that suggestion occurs in the celebrated La Vallière catalogue, in which a MS. "Dance of Death" is described, with the note, "On l'a dit composé par un nommé Macabre." That the spirit of German satire of the period did actually run in that direction, both poetically and pictorially, is proved by the works of Sebastian Brandt, whose "Ship of Fools," in which personifications of all the leading types of human folly are represented as embarked in the Ship of Life, is an allegory closely resembling, in many respects, the "Dance of Death," while its profuse illustrations are not very dissimilar in general spirit to those belonging to that subject. It is worthy of note, also, that the "Ship of Fools" was translated from the German into French as "La Nef des Fous," and was soon followed by a companion work devoted exclusively to women, under the title of "La Nef des Folles," just as the first edition of the "Dance of Death," which was printed in France under the name of "La Danse Macabre," was as immediately followed by "La Danse Macabre des Femmes." Nevertheless, it does not appear probable that the term Macabre originated in Germany. The supposition that the name of the German poet was Macabre is, indeed, far less probable than that he might have named the poem after St. Macarius, while neither hypothesis is borne out by the known facts of the case, for we do not find a single German version bearing the title of "Macabre," or "Macabrean," but simply that of the "Doden Dänze," or "Todten Taenze." Was it, then, a French author who composed the poem? and, if so, was the title founded upon the name of St. Macarius, or derived from some other source? Van Prael suggested that Magbar and Magbarah* were Arabic names for a cemetery; and this is possibly a hint that may eventually lead to a more satisfactory explanation of the term than that founded on the name of St. Macarius, and there is collateral evidence of some weight that may be brought forward in support of this view. It is well known that Nicholas Flamel, who lived in the last half of the 14th century, and who enjoyed the various reputation of author, merchant, alchemist, and astrologer, was also a munificent benefactor of

* The Bibliophile Jacob ridicules this derivation, and jocosely suggests in its stead *Abracadabra.*

entitled "Van drén Konygen," and "Van den doden Konigen, und van den levenden Konigen." There were also English versions of the legend, one of which is preserved among the Arundel manuscripts in the British Museum. This English version of the "Three Living and the Three Dead," in addition to the interest of the subject, is remarkable as affording a curious example of the English language in a transition state. For instance, in the rude illumination at the beginning three kings, who are represented as pursuing the exciting amusement of the chase in a pleasant wood, suddenly meet three skeletons, at the sight of which, being naturally struck with dismay, the first king is represented as saying,—

> Ich am afert, lo what ich se
> Me thinketh hit beth develes thre ;

to which the first skeleton replies,—

> Ich wes wel fair—such skelton be—
> For Godes love be wer by me ;

which, put into rather more modern form, would read,—

> I am afeard !—lo ! what d'I see ?
> Methinks that it be devils three ;

the response being,—

> I, once well fair, now skel(e)ton be ;
> For God's love, then, be warned by me.

The characters of this legend are often changed in the different versions ; sometimes they are a king, a queen, and a nobleman ; sometimes three noble youths in gaily-broidered suits, and bearing richly-adorned weapons, revelling, as hunters, in the luxuries and privileges of rank and wealth. There is a very early representation of this version of the "Three Living and the Three Dead" in the church at Brie, near Metz.

Orcagna's celebrated "Triumph of Death" in the Campo Santo, at Pisa, painted in the 14th century, may be called an Italianized version of this legend. The three principal figures are the three kings of the original legend, but they are accompanied by their mistresses, and St. Macarius himself takes the place of the three skeletons, showing to the living kings three open graves, in which lie the bodies of three dead kings. In another part of the composition Death is symbolized by a female figure furnished with bats' wings and claws, and bearing a scythe, with which she sweeps down popes, emperors, kings, and others of all classes.

Here, then, we already find an extension of the range of the legend of St. Macarius to all classes, as carried out more definitely and distinctly in the "Dance of Death," which no doubt owed much of its immediate and lasting popularity, as previously suggested, to its fearless carrying out, in a more modern and expressive form, of the well-known verses of Horace—

> Pallida mors æquo pulsat pede pauperum tabernas,
> Regumque turres.

The more Northern expansion of this subject, whether we consider it as a series of stanzas forming a poem entitled "The Dance of Death," or as

a mere extension of the legend of St. Macarius, or as an original and more extensive work of analogous character, to which new verses were added from time to time as fresh characters were introduced, is asserted to have been of German origin,—a conclusion arrived at from the fact that the French and Latin verses attached to the earliest printed editions of the "Dance of Death" are stated, in more than one of the short prefaces or titles attached to those works, to have been translated from the German. On the other hand, with a view to explain the meaning of the term "Macabre," under which the first editions of the "Dance of Death" were issued in France, a few observations of an apparently opposite tendency may be conveniently made in this place. Firstly, if a German author either extended the poem of St. Macarius, or composed another of analogous but more extensive character, it seems probable that he would, or might, have founded his title on the name of the original author, and have termed his work the Macarian or Machabrian Dance, as some writers on the subject have suggested ; and an allusion closely bordering upon that suggestion occurs in the celebrated La Vallière catalogue, in which a MS. "Dance of Death" is described, with the note, "On l'a dit composé par un nommé Macabre." That the spirit of German satire of the period did actually run in that direction, both poetically and pictorially, is proved by the works of Sebastian Brandt, whose "Ship of Fools," in which personifications of all the leading types of human folly are represented as embarked in the Ship of Life, is an allegory closely resembling, in many respects, the "Dance of Death," while its profuse illustrations are not very dissimilar in general spirit to those belonging to that subject. It is worthy of note, also, that the "Ship of Fools" was translated from the German into French as "La Nef des Fous," and was soon followed by a. companion work devoted exclusively to women, under the title of "La Nef des Folles," just as the first edition of the "Dance of Death," which was printed in France under the name of "La Danse Macabre," was as immediately followed by "La Danse Macabre des Femmes." Nevertheless, it does not appear probable that the term Macabre originated in Germany. The supposition that the name of the German poet was Macabre is, indeed, far less probable than that he might have named the poem after St. Macarius, while neither hypothesis is borne out by the known facts of the case, for we do not find a single German version bearing the title of "Macabre," or "Macabrean," but simply that of the "Doden Dänze," or "Todten Taenze." Was it, then, a French author who composed the poem? and, if so, was the title founded upon the name of St. Macarius, or derived from some other source? Van Prael suggested that Magbar and Magbarah* were Arabic names for a cemetery; and this is possibly a hint that may eventually lead to a more satisfactory explanation of the term than that founded on the name of St. Macarius, and there is collateral evidence of some weight that may be brought forward in support of this view. It is well known that Nicholas Flamel, who lived in the last half of the 14th century, and who enjoyed the various reputation of author, merchant, alchemist, and astrologer, was also a munificent benefactor of

* The Bibliophile Jacob ridicules this derivation, and jocosely suggests in its stead *Abracadabra.*

entitled "Van drén Konygen," and "Van den doden Konigen, und van den levenden Konigen." There were also English versions of the legend, one of which is preserved among the Arundel manuscripts in the British Museum. This English version of the "Three Living and the Three Dead," in addition to the interest of the subject, is remarkable as affording a curious example of the English language in a transition state. For instance, in the rude illumination at the beginning three kings, who are represented as pursuing the exciting amusement of the chase in a pleasant wood, suddenly meet three skeletons, at the sight of which, being naturally struck with dismay, the first king is represented as saying,—

> Ich am afert, lo what ich se
> Me thinketh hit beth develes thre ;

to which the first skeleton replies,—

> Ich wes wel fair—such skelton be—
> For Godes love be wer by me ;

which, put into rather more modern form, would read,—

> I am afeard !—lo ! what d'I see ?
> Methinks that it be devils three ;

the response being,—

> I, once well fair, now skel(e)ton be ;
> For God's love, then, be warned by me.

The characters of this legend are often changed in the different versions ; sometimes they are a king, a queen, and a nobleman ; sometimes three noble youths in gaily-broidered suits, and bearing richly-adorned weapons, revelling, as hunters, in the luxuries and privileges of rank and wealth. There is a very early representation of this version of the "Three Living and the Three Dead" in the church at Brie, near Metz.

Orcagna's celebrated "Triumph of Death" in the Campo Santo, at Pisa, painted in the 14th century, may be called an Italianized version of this legend. The three principal figures are the three kings of the original legend, but they are accompanied by their mistresses, and St. Macarius himself takes the place of the three skeletons, showing to the living kings three open graves, in which lie the bodies of three dead kings. In another part of the composition Death is symbolized by a female figure furnished with bats' wings and claws, and bearing a scythe, with which she sweeps down popes, emperors, kings, and others of all classes.

Here, then, we already find an extension of the range of the legend of St. Macarius to all classes, as carried out more definitely and distinctly in the "Dance of Death," which no doubt owed much of its immediate and lasting popularity, as previously suggested, to its fearless carrying out, in a more modern and expressive form, of the well-known verses of Horace—

> Pallida mors æquo pulsat pede pauperum tabernas,
> Regumque turres.

The more Northern expansion of this subject, whether we consider it as a series of stanzas forming a poem entitled "The Dance of Death," or as

a mere extension of the legend of St. Macarius, or as an original and more extensive work of analogous character, to which new verses were added from time to time as fresh characters were introduced, is asserted to have been of German origin,—a conclusion arrived at from the fact that the French and Latin verses attached to the earliest printed editions of the "Dance of Death" are stated, in more than one of the short prefaces or titles attached to those works, to have been translated from the German. On the other hand, with a view to explain the meaning of the term "Macabre," under which the first editions of the "Dance of Death" were issued in France, a few observations of an apparently opposite tendency may be conveniently made in this place. Firstly, if a German author either extended the poem of St. Macarius, or composed another of analogous but more extensive character, it seems probable that he would, or might, have founded his title on the name of the original author, and have termed his work the Macarian or Machabrian Dance, as some writers on the subject have suggested ; and an allusion closely bordering upon that suggestion occurs in the celebrated La Vallière catalogue, in which a MS. "Dance of Death" is described, with the note, "On l'a dit composé par un nommé Macabre." That the spirit of German satire of the period did actually run in that direction, both poetically and pictorially, is proved by the works of Sebastian Brandt, whose "Ship of Fools," in which personifications of all the leading types of human folly are represented as embarked in the Ship of Life, is an allegory closely resembling, in many respects, the "Dance of Death," while its profuse illustrations are not very dissimilar in general spirit to those belonging to that subject. It is worthy of note, also, that the "Ship of Fools" was translated from the German into French as "La Nef des Fous," and was suon followed by a companion work devoted exclusively to women, under the title of "La Nef des Folles," just as the first edition of the "Dance of Death," which was printed in France under the name of "La Danse Macabre," was as immediately followed by "La Danse Macabre des Femmes." Nevertheless, it does not appear probable that the term Macabre originated in Germany. The supposition that the name of the German poet was Macabre is, indeed, far less probable than that he might have named the poem after St. Macarius, while neither hypothesis is borne out by the known facts of the case, for we do not find a single German version bearing the title of "Macabre," or "Macabrean," but simply that of the "Doden Dänze," or "Todten Taenze." Was it, then, a French author who composed the poem? and, if so, was the title founded upon the name of St. Macarius, or derived from some other source? Van Prael suggested that Magbar and Magbarah* were Arabic names for a cemetery; and this is possibly a hint that may eventually lead to a more satisfactory explanation of the term than that founded on the name of St. Macarius, and there is collateral evidence of some weight that may be brought forward in support of this view. It is well known that Nicholas Flamel, who lived in the last half of the 14th century, and who enjoyed the various reputation of author, merchant, alchemist, and astrologer, was also a munificent benefactor of

---

* The Bibliophile Jacob ridicules this derivation, and jocosely suggests in its stead *Abracadabra.*

entitled "Van drén Konygen," and "Van den doden Konigen, und van den levenden Konigen." There were also English versions of the legend, one of which is preserved among the Arundel manuscripts in the British Museum. This English version of the "Three Living and the Three Dead," in addition to the interest of the subject, is remarkable as affording a curious example of the English language in a transition state. For instance, in the rude illumination at the beginning three kings, who are represented as pursuing the exciting amusement of the chase in a pleasant wood, suddenly meet three skeletons, at the sight of which, being naturally struck with dismay, the first king is represented as saying,—

> Ich am afert, lo what ich se
> Me thinketh hit beth develes thre ;

to which the first skeleton replies,—

> Ich wes wel fair—such skelton be—
> For Godes love be wer by me ;

which, put into rather more modern form, would read,—

> I am afeard !—lo ! what d'I see ?
> Methinks that it be devils three ;

the response being,—

> I, once well fair, now skel(e)ton be ;
> For God's love, then, be warned by me.

The characters of this legend are often changed in the different versions ; sometimes they are a king, a queen, and a nobleman ; sometimes three noble youths in gaily-broidered suits, and bearing richly-adorned weapons, revelling, as hunters, in the luxuries and privileges of rank and wealth. There is a very early representation of this version of the "Three Living and the Three Dead " in the church at Brie, near Metz.

Orcagna's celebrated " Triumph of Death " in the Campo Santo, at Pisa, painted in the 14th century, may be called an Italianized version of this legend. The three principal figures are the three kings of the original legend, but they are accompanied by their mistresses, and St. Macarius himself takes the place of the three skeletons, showing to the living kings three open graves, in which lie the bodies of three dead kings. In another part of the composition Death is symbolized by a female figure furnished with bats' wings and claws, and bearing a scythe, with which she sweeps down popes, emperors, kings, and others of all classes.

Here, then, we already find an extension of the range of the legend of St. Macarius to all classes, as carried out more definitely and distinctly in the "Dance of Death," which no doubt owed much of its immediate and lasting popularity, as previously suggested, to its fearless carrying out, in a more modern and expressive form, of the well-known verses of Horace—

> Pallida mors æquo pulsat pede pauperum tabernas,
> Regumque turres.

a mere extension of the legend of St. Macarius, or as an original and
more extensive work of analogous character, to which new verses were added
from time to time as fresh characters were introduced, is asserted to have
been of German origin,—a conclusion arrived at from the fact that the
French and Latin verses attached to the earliest printed editions of the
"Dance of Death" are stated, in more than one of the short prefaces or
titles attached to those works, to have been translated from the German.
On the other hand, with a view to explain the meaning of the term
"Macabre," under which the first editions of the "Dance of Death" were
issued in France, a few observations of an apparently opposite tendency
may be conveniently made in this place. Firstly, if a German author
either extended the poem of St. Macarius, or composed another of analogous but more extensive character, it seems probable that he would, or
might, have founded his title on the name of the original author, and have
termed his work the Macarian or Machabrian Dance, as some writers
on the subject have suggested; and an allusion closely bordering upon that
suggestion occurs in the celebrated La Vallière catalogue, in which a
MS. "Dance of Death" is described, with the note, "On l'a dit composé
par un nommé Macabre." That the spirit of German satire of the period
did actually run in that direction, both poetically and pictorially, is proved
by the works of Sebastian Brandt, whose "Ship of Fools," in which personifications of all the leading types of human folly are represented as
embarked in the Ship of Life, is an allegory closely resembling, in many
respects, the "Dance of Death," while its profuse illustrations are not
very dissimilar in general spirit to those belonging to that subject. It is
worthy of note, also, that the "Ship of Fools" was translated from
the German into French as "La Nef des Fous," and was soon followed
by a companion work devoted exclusively to women, under the title of
"La Nef des Folles," just as the first edition of the "Dance of Death,"
which was printed in France under the name of "La Danse Macabre,"
was as immediately followed by "La Danse Macabre des Femmes."
Nevertheless, it does not appear probable that the term Macabre originated
in Germany. The supposition that the name of the German poet was
Macabre is, indeed, far less probable than that he might have named the
poem after St. Macarius, while neither hypothesis is borne out by the
known facts of the case, for we do not find a single German version bearing
the title of "Macabre," or "Macabrean," but simply that of the "Doden
Dänze," or "Todten Taenze." Was it, then, a French author who composed the poem? and, if so, was the title founded upon the name of
St. Macarius, or derived from some other source? Van Prael suggested
that Magbar and Magbarah* were Arabic names for a cemetery; and this is
possibly a hint that may eventually lead to a more satisfactory explanation
of the term than that founded on the name of St. Macarius, and there is
collateral evidence of some weight that may be brought forward in support
of this view. It is well known that Nicholas Flamel, who lived in the last
half of the 14th century, and who enjoyed the various reputation of author,
merchant, alchemist, and astrologer, was also a munificent benefactor of

* The Bibliophile Jacob ridicules this derivation, and jocosely suggests in its stead
Abracadabra.

entitled "Van drén Konygen," and "Van den doden Konigen, und van
den levenden Konigen." There were also English versions of the legend,
one of which is preserved among the Arundel manuscripts in the British
Museum. This English version of the "Three Living and the Three
Dead," in addition to the interest of the subject, is remarkable as affording
a curious example of the English language in a transition state.   For
instance, in the rude illumination at the beginning three kings, who are
represented as pursuing the exciting amusement of the chase in a pleasant
wood, suddenly meet three skeletons, at the sight of which, being naturally
struck with dismay, the first king is represented as saying,—

> Ich am afert, lo what ich se
> Me thinketh hit beth develes thre ;

to which the first skeleton replies,—

> Ich wes wel fair—such skelton be—
> For Godes love be wer by me ;

which, put into rather more modern form, would read,—

> I am afeard !—lo ! what d'I see?
> Methinks that it be devils three ;

the response being,—

> I, once well fair, now skel(e)ton be ;
> For God's love, then, be warned by me.

The characters of this legend are often changed in the different versions ;
sometimes they are a king, a queen, and a nobleman ; sometimes three
noble youths in gaily-broidered suits, and bearing richly-adorned weapons,
revelling, as hunters, in the luxuries and privileges of rank and wealth.
There is a very early representation of this version of the "Three Living
and the Three Dead" in the church at Brie, near Metz.

Orcagna's celebrated "Triumph of Death" in the Campo Santo, at Pisa,
painted in the 14th century, may be called an Italianized version of this
legend. The three principal figures are the three kings of the original legend,
but they are accompanied by their mistresses, and St. Macarius himself
takes the place of the three skeletons, showing to the living kings three open
graves, in which lie the bodies of three dead kings.   In another part of the
composition Death is symbolized by a female figure furnished with bats'
wings and claws, and bearing a scythe, with which she sweeps down popes,
emperors, kings, and others of all classes.

Here, then, we already find an extension of the range of the legend of
St. Macarius to all classes, as carried out more definitely and distinctly
in the "Dance of Death," which no doubt owed much of its immediate
and lasting popularity, as previously suggested, to its fearless carrying out,
in a more modern and expressive form, of the well-known verses of Horace—

> Pallida mors æquo pulsat pede pauperum tabernas,
> Regumque turres.

The more Northern expansion of this subject, whether we consider it as
a series of stanzas forming a poem entitled "The Dance of Death," or as

a mere extension of the legend of St. Macarius, or as an original and more extensive work of analogous character, to which new verses were added from time to time as fresh characters were introduced, is asserted to have been of German origin,—a conclusion arrived at from the fact that the French and Latin verses attached to the earliest printed editions of the "Dance of Death" are stated, in more than one of the short prefaces or titles attached to those works, to have been translated from the German. On the other hand, with a view to explain the meaning of the term "Macabre," under which the first editions of the "Dance of Death" were issued in France, a few observations of an apparently opposite tendency may be conveniently made in this place. Firstly, if a German author either extended the poem of St. Macarius, or composed another of analogous but more extensive character, it seems probable that he would, or might, have founded his title on the name of the original author, and have termed his work the Macarian or Machabrian Dance, as some writers on the subject have suggested; and an allusion closely bordering upon that suggestion occurs in the celebrated La Vallière catalogue, in which a MS. "Dance of Death" is described, with the note, "On l'a dit composé par un nommé Macabre." That the spirit of German satire of the period did actually run in that direction, both poetically and pictorially, is proved by the works of Sebastian Brandt, whose "Ship of Fools," in which personifications of all the leading types of human folly are represented as embarked in the Ship of Life, is an allegory closely resembling, in many respects, the "Dance of Death," while its profuse illustrations are not very dissimilar in general spirit to those belonging to that subject. It is worthy of note, also, that the "Ship of Fools" was translated from the German into French as "La Nef des Fous," and was soon followed by a companion work devoted exclusively to women, under the title of "La Nef des Folles," just as the first edition of the "Dance of Death," which was printed in France under the name of "La Danse Macabre," was as immediately followed by "La Danse Macabre des Femmes." Nevertheless, it does not appear probable that the term Macabre originated in Germany. The supposition that the name of the German poet was Macabre is, indeed, far less probable than that he might have named the poem after St. Macarius, while neither hypothesis is borne out by the known facts of the case, for we do not find a single German version bearing the title of "Macabre," or "Macabrean," but simply that of the "Doden Dänze," or "Todten Taenze." Was it, then, a French author who composed the poem? and, if so, was the title founded upon the name of St. Macarius, or derived from some other source? Van Prael suggested that Magbar and Magbarah* were Arabic names for a cemetery; and this is possibly a hint that may eventually lead to a more satisfactory explanation of the term than that founded on the name of St. Macarius, and there is collateral evidence of some weight that may be brought forward in support of this view. It is well known that Nicholas Flamel, who lived in the last half of the 14th century, and who enjoyed the various reputation of author, merchant, alchemist, and astrologer, was also a munificent benefactor of

* The Bibliophile Jacob ridicules this derivation, and jocosely suggests in its stead *Abracadabra.*

entitled "Van drén Konygen," and "Van den doden Konigen, und van
den levenden Konigen." There were also English versions of the legend,
one of which is preserved among the Arundel manuscripts in the British
Museum. This English version of the "Three Living and the Three
Dead," in addition to the interest of the subject, is remarkable as affording
a curious example of the English language in a transition state. For
instance, in the rude illumination at the beginning three kings, who are
represented as pursuing the exciting amusement of the chase in a pleasant
wood, suddenly meet three skeletons, at the sight of which, being naturally
struck with dismay, the first king is represented as saying,—

> Ich am afert, lo what ich se
> Me thinketh hit beth develes thre ;

to which the first skeleton replies,—

> Ich wes wel fair—such skelton be—
> For Godes love be wer by me ;

which, put into rather more modern form, would read,—

> I am afeard !—lo ! what d'I see ?
> Methinks that it be devils three ;

the response being,—

> I, once well fair, now skel(e)ton be ;
> For God's love, then, be warned by me.

The characters of this legend are often changed in the different versions ;
sometimes they are a king, a queen, and a nobleman ; sometimes three
noble youths in gaily-broidered suits, and bearing richly-adorned weapons,
revelling, as hunters, in the luxuries and privileges of rank and wealth.
There is a very early representation of this version of the "Three Living
and the Three Dead" in the church at Brie, near Metz.

Orcagna's celebrated "Triumph of Death" in the Campo Santo, at Pisa,
painted in the 14th century, may be called an Italianized version of this
legend. The three principal figures are the three kings of the original legend,
but they are accompanied by their mistresses, and St. Macarius himself
takes the place of the three skeletons, showing to the living kings three open
graves, in which lie the bodies of three dead kings. In another part of the
composition Death is symbolized by a female figure furnished with bats'
wings and claws, and bearing a scythe, with which she sweeps down popes,
emperors, kings, and others of all classes.

Here, then, we already find an extension of the range of the legend of
St. Macarius to all classes, as carried out more definitely and distinctly
in the "Dance of Death," which no doubt owed much of its immediate
and lasting popularity, as previously suggested, to its fearless carrying out,
in a more modern and expressive form, of the well-known verses of Horace—

> Pallida mors æquo pulsat pede pauperum tabernas,
> Regumque turres.

The more Northern expansion of this subject, whether we consider it as
a series of stanzas forming a poem entitled "The Dance of Death," or as

a mere extension of the legend of St. Macarius, or as an original and more extensive work of analogous character, to which new verses were added from time to time as fresh characters were introduced, is asserted to have been of German origin,—a conclusion arrived at from the fact that the French and Latin verses attached to the earliest printed editions of the "Dance of Death" are stated, in more than one of the short prefaces or titles attached to those works, to have been translated from the German. On the other hand, with a view to explain the meaning of the term "Macabre," under which the first editions of the "Dance of Death" were issued in France, a few observations of an apparently opposite tendency may be conveniently made in this place. Firstly, if a German author either extended the poem of St. Macarius, or composed another of analogous but more extensive character, it seems probable that he would, or might, have founded his title on the name of the original author, and have termed his work the Macarian or Machabrian Dance, as some writers on the subject have suggested; and an allusion closely bordering upon that suggestion occurs in the celebrated La Vallière catalogue, in which a MS. "Dance of Death" is described, with the note, "On l'a dit composé par un nommé Macabre." That the spirit of German satire of the period did actually run in that direction, both poetically and pictorially, is proved by the works of Sebastian Brandt, whose "Ship of Fools," in which personifications of all the leading types of human folly are represented as embarked in the Ship of Life, is an allegory closely resembling, in many respects, the "Dance of Death," while its profuse illustrations are not very dissimilar in general spirit to those belonging to that subject. It is worthy of note, also, that the "Ship of Fools" was translated from the German into French as "La Nef des Fous," and was soon followed by a. companion work devoted exclusively to women, under the title of "La Nef des Folles," just as the first edition of the "Dance of Death," which was printed in France under the name of "La Danse Macabre," was as immediately followed by "La Danse Macabre des Femmes." Nevertheless, it does not appear probable that the term Macabre originated in Germany. The supposition that the name of the German poet was Macabre is, indeed, far less probable than that he might have named the poem after St. Macarius, while neither hypothesis is borne out by the known facts of the case, for we do not find a single German version bearing the title of "Macabre," or "Macabrean," but simply that of the "Doden Dänze," or "Todten Taenze." Was it, then, a French author who composed the poem? and, if so, was the title founded upon the name of St. Macarius, or derived from some other source? Van Prael suggested that Magbar and Magbarah* were Arabic names for a cemetery; and this is possibly a hint that may eventually lead to a more satisfactory explanation of the term than that founded on the name of St. Macarius, and there is collateral evidence of some weight that may be brought forward in support of this view. It is well known that Nicholas Flamel, who lived in the last half of the 14th century, and who enjoyed the various reputation of author, merchant, alchemist, and astrologer, was also a munificent benefactor of

* The Bibliophile Jacob ridicules this derivation, and jocosely suggests in its stead *Abracadabra.*

entitled "Van drén Konygen," and "Van den doden Konigen, und van
den levenden Konigen."   There were also English versions of the legend,
one of which is preserved among the Arundel manuscripts in the British
Museum.   This English version of the "Three Living and the Three
Dead," in addition to the interest of the subject, is remarkable as affording
a curious example of the English language in a transition state.   For
instance, in the rude illumination at the beginning three kings, who are
represented as pursuing the exciting amusement of the chase in a pleasant
wood, suddenly meet three skeletons, at the sight of which, being naturally
struck with dismay, the first king is represented as saying,—

> Ich am afert, lo what ich se
> Me thinketh hit beth develes thre ;

to which the first skeleton replies,—

> Ich wes wel fair—such skelton be—
> For Godes love be wer by me ;

which, put into rather more modern form, would read,—

> I am afeard !—lo ! what d'I see ?
> Methinks that it be devils three ;

the response being,—

> I, once well fair, now skel(e)ton be ;
> For God's love, then, be warned by me.

The characters of this legend are often changed in the different versions ;
sometimes they are a king, a queen, and a nobleman ; sometimes three
noble youths in gaily-broidered suits, and bearing richly-adorned weapons,
revelling, as hunters, in the luxuries and privileges of rank and wealth.
There is a very early representation of this version of the "Three Living
and the Three Dead " in the church at Brie, near Metz.

Orcagna's celebrated " Triumph of Death " in the Campo Santo, at Pisa,
painted in the 14th century, may be called an Italianized version of this
legend. The three principal figures are the three kings of the original legend,
but they are accompanied by their mistresses, and St. Macarius himself
takes the place of the three skeletons, showing to the living kings three open
graves, in which lie the bodies of three dead kings.   In another part of the
composition Death is symbolized by a female figure furnished with bats'
wings and claws, and bearing a scythe, with which she sweeps down popes,
emperors, kings, and others of all classes.

Here, then, we already find an extension of the range of the legend of
St. Macarius to all classes, as carried out more definitely and distinctly
in the "Dance of Death," which no doubt owed much of its immediate
and lasting popularity, as previously suggested, to its fearless carrying out,
in a more modern and expressive form, of the well-known verses of Horace—

> Pallida mors æquo pulsat pede pauperum tabernas,
> Regumque turres.

The more Northern expansion of this subject, whether we consider it as
a series of stanzas forming a poem entitled "The Dance of Death," or as

a mere extension of the legend of St. Macarius, or as an original and more extensive work of analogous character, to which new verses were added from time to time as fresh characters were introduced, is asserted to have been of German origin,—a conclusion arrived at from the fact that the French and Latin verses attached to the earliest printed editions of the "Dance of Death" are stated, in more than one of the short prefaces or titles attached to those works, to have been translated from the German. On the other hand, with a view to explain the meaning of the term "Macabre," under which the first editions of the "Dance of Death" were issued in France, a few observations of an apparently opposite tendency may be conveniently made in this place. Firstly, if a German author either extended the poem of St. Macarius, or composed another of analogous but more extensive character, it seems probable that he would, or might, have founded his title on the name of the original author, and have termed his work the Macarian or Machabrian Dance, as some writers on the subject have suggested ; and an allusion closely bordering upon that suggestion occurs in the celebrated La Vallière catalogue, in which a MS. "Dance of Death" is described, with the note, "On l'a dit composé par un nommé Macabre." That the spirit of German satire of the period did actually run in that direction, both poetically and pictorially, is proved by the works of Sebastian Brandt, whose "Ship of Fools," in which personifications of all the leading types of human folly are represented as embarked in the Ship of Life, is an allegory closely resembling, in many respects, the "Dance of Death," while its profuse illustrations are not very dissimilar in general spirit to those belonging to that subject. It is worthy of note, also, that the "Ship of Fools" was translated from the German into French as "La Nef des Fous," and was soon followed by a companion work devoted exclusively to women, under the title of "La Nef des Folles," just as the first edition of the "Dance of Death," which was printed in France under the name of "La Danse Macabre," was as immediately followed by "La Danse Macabre des Femmes." Nevertheless, it does not appear probable that the term Macabre originated in Germany. The supposition that the name of the German poet was Macabre is, indeed, far less probable than that he might have named the poem after St. Macarius, while neither hypothesis is borne out by the known facts of the case, for we do not find a single German version bearing the title of "Macabre," or "Macabrean," but simply that of the "Doden Dänze," or "Todten Taenze." Was it, then, a French author who composed the poem? and, if so, was the title founded upon the name of St. Macarius, or derived from some other source? Van Prael suggested that Magbar and Magbarah* were Arabic names for a cemetery; and this is possibly a hint that may eventually lead to a more satisfactory explanation of the term than that founded on the name of St. Macarius, and there is collateral evidence of some weight that may be brought forward in support of this view. It is well known that Nicholas Flamel, who lived in the last half of the 14th century, and who enjoyed the various reputation of author, merchant, alchemist, and astrologer, was also a munificent benefactor of

* The Bibliophile Jacob ridicules this derivation, and jocosely suggests in its stead *Abracadabra.*

entitled "Van drén Konygen," and "Van den doden Konigen, und van den levenden Konigen." There were also English versions of the legend, one of which is preserved among the Arundel manuscripts in the British Museum. This English version of the "Three Living and the Three Dead," in addition to the interest of the subject, is remarkable as affording a curious example of the English language in a transition state. For instance, in the rude illumination at the beginning three kings, who are represented as pursuing the exciting amusement of the chase in a pleasant wood, suddenly meet three skeletons, at the sight of which, being naturally struck with dismay, the first king is represented as saying,—

> Ich am afert, lo what ich se
> Me thinketh hit beth develes thre ;

to which the first skeleton replies,—

> Ich wes wel fair—such skelton be—
> For Godes love be wer by me ;

which, put into rather more modern form, would read,—

> I am afeard !—lo ! what d'I see ?
> Methinks that it be devils three ;

the response being,—

> I, once well fair, now skel(e)ton be ;
> For God's love, then, be warned by me.

The characters of this legend are often changed in the different versions ; sometimes they are a king, a queen, and a nobleman ; sometimes three noble youths in gaily-broidered suits, and bearing richly-adorned weapons, revelling, as hunters, in the luxuries and privileges of rank and wealth. There is a very early representation of this version of the "Three Living and the Three Dead" in the church at Brie, near Metz.

Orcagna's celebrated "Triumph of Death" in the Campo Santo, at Pisa, painted in the 14th century, may be called an Italianized version of this legend. The three principal figures are the three kings of the original legend, but they are accompanied by their mistresses, and St. Macarius himself takes the place of the three skeletons, showing to the living kings three open graves, in which lie the bodies of three dead kings. In another part of the composition Death is symbolized by a female figure furnished with bats' wings and claws, and bearing a scythe, with which she sweeps down popes, emperors, kings, and others of all classes.

Here, then, we already find an extension of the range of the legend of St. Macarius to all classes, as carried out more definitely and distinctly in the "Dance of Death," which no doubt owed much of its immediate and lasting popularity, as previously suggested, to its fearless carrying out, in a more modern and expressive form, of the well-known verses of Horace—

> Pallida mors æquo pulsat pede pauperum tabernas,
> Regumque turres.

The more Northern expansion of this subject, whether we consider it as a series of stanzas forming a poem entitled "The Dance of Death," or as

a mere extension of the legend of St. Macarius, or as an original and more extensive work of analogous character, to which new verses were added from time to time as fresh characters were introduced, is asserted to have been of German origin,—a conclusion arrived at from the fact that the French and Latin verses attached to the earliest printed editions of the "Dance of Death" are stated, in more than one of the short prefaces or titles attached to those works, to have been translated from the German. On the other hand, with a view to explain the meaning of the term "Macabre," under which the first editions of the "Dance of Death" were issued in France, a few observations of an apparently opposite tendency may be conveniently made in this place. Firstly, if a German author either extended the poem of St. Macarius, or composed another of analogous but more extensive character, it seems probable that he would, or might, have founded his title on the name of the original author, and have termed his work the Macarian or Machabrian Dance, as some writers on the subject have suggested; and an allusion closely bordering upon that suggestion occurs in the celebrated La Vallière catalogue, in which a MS. "Dance of Death" is described, with the note, "On l'a dit composé par un nommé Macabre." That the spirit of German satire of the period did actually run in that direction, both poetically and pictorially, is proved by the works of Sebastian Brandt, whose "Ship of Fools," in which personifications of all the leading types of human folly are represented as embarked in the Ship of Life, is an allegory closely resembling, in many respects, the "Dance of Death," while its profuse illustrations are not very dissimilar in general spirit to those belonging to that subject. It is worthy of note, also, that the "Ship of Fools" was translated from the German into French as "La Nef des Fous," and was soon followed by a companion work devoted exclusively to women, under the title of "La Nef des Folles," just as the first edition of the "Dance of Death," which was printed in France under the name of "La Danse Macabre," was as immediately followed by "La Danse Macabre des Femmes." Nevertheless, it does not appear probable that the term Macabre originated in Germany. The supposition that the name of the German poet was Macabre is, indeed, far less probable than that he might have named the poem after St. Macarius, while neither hypothesis is borne out by the known facts of the case, for we do not find a single German version bearing the title of "Macabre," or "Macabrean," but simply that of the "Doden Dänze," or "Todten Taenze." Was it, then, a French author who composed the poem? and, if so, was the title founded upon the name of St. Macarius, or derived from some other source? Van Prael suggested that Magbar and Magbarah* were Arabic names for a cemetery; and this is possibly a hint that may eventually lead to a more satisfactory explanation of the term than that founded on the name of St. Macarius, and there is collateral evidence of some weight that may be brought forward in support of this view. It is well known that Nicholas Flamel, who lived in the last half of the 14th century, and who enjoyed the various reputation of author, merchant, alchemist, and astrologer, was also a munificent benefactor of

---

* The Bibliophile Jacob ridicules this derivation, and jocosely suggests in its stead *Abracadabra.*

entitled "Van drén Konygen," and "Van den doden Konigen, und van den levenden Konigen." There were also English versions of the legend, one of which is preserved among the Arundel manuscripts in the British Museum. This English version of the "Three Living and the Three Dead," in addition to the interest of the subject, is remarkable as affording a curious example of the English language in a transition state. For instance, in the rude illumination at the beginning three kings, who are represented as pursuing the exciting amusement of the chase in a pleasant wood, suddenly meet three skeletons, at the sight of which, being naturally struck with dismay, the first king is represented as saying,—

> Ich am afert, lo what ich se
> Me thinketh hit beth develes thre ;

to which the first skeleton replies,—

> Ich wes wel fair—such skelton be—
> For Godes love be wer by me ;

which, put into rather more modern form, would read,—

> I am afeard !—lo ! what d'l see ?
> Methinks that it be devils three ;

the response being,—

> I, once well fair, now skel(e)ton be ;
> For God's love, then, be warned by me.

The characters of this legend are often changed in the different versions ; sometimes they are a king, a queen, and a nobleman ; sometimes three noble youths in gaily-broidered suits, and bearing richly-adorned weapons, revelling, as hunters, in the luxuries and privileges of rank and wealth. There is a very early representation of this version of the "Three Living and the Three Dead" in the church at Brie, near Metz.

Orcagna's celebrated "Triumph of Death" in the Campo Santo, at Pisa, painted in the 14th century, may be called an Italianized version of this legend. The three principal figures are the three kings of the original legend, but they are accompanied by their mistresses, and St. Macarius himself takes the place of the three skeletons, showing to the living kings three open graves, in which lie the bodies of three dead kings. In another part of the composition Death is symbolized by a female figure furnished with bats' wings and claws, and bearing a scythe, with which she sweeps down popes, emperors, kings, and others of all classes.

Here, then, we already find an extension of the range of the legend of St. Macarius to all classes, as carried out more definitely and distinctly in the "Dance of Death," which no doubt owed much of its immediate and lasting popularity, as previously suggested, to its fearless carrying out, in a more modern and expressive form, of the well-known verses of Horace—

> Pallida mors æquo pulsat pede pauperum tabernas,
> Regumque turres.

The more Northern expansion of this subject, whether we consider it as a series of stanzas forming a poem entitled "The Dance of Death," or as

a mere extension of the legend of St. Macarius, or as an original and more extensive work of analogous character, to which new verses were added from time to time as fresh characters were introduced, is asserted to have been of German origin,—a conclusion arrived at from the fact that the French and Latin verses attached to the earliest printed editions of the " Dance of Death " are stated, in more than one of the short prefaces or titles attached to those works, to have been translated from the German. On the other hand, with a view to explain the meaning of the term " Macabre," under which the first editions of the " Dance of Death " were issued in France, a few observations of an apparently opposite tendency may be conveniently made in this place.   Firstly, if a German author either extended the poem of St. Macarius, or composed another of analogous but more extensive character, it seems probable that he would, or might, have founded his title on the name of the original author, and have termed his work the Macarian or Machabrian Dance, as some writers on the subject have suggested; and an allusion closely bordering upon that suggestion occurs in the celebrated La Vallière catalogue, in which a MS. " Dance of Death " is described, with the note, " On l'a dit composé par un nommé Macabre."   That the spirit of German satire of the period did actually run in that direction, both poetically and pictorially, is proved by the works of Sebastian Brandt, whose " Ship of Fools," in which personifications of all the leading types of human folly are represented as embarked in the Ship of Life, is an allegory closely resembling, in many respects, the " Dance of Death," while its profuse illustrations are not very dissimilar in general spirit to those belonging to that subject.   It is worthy of note, also, that the " Ship of Fools " was translated from the German into French as " La Nef des Fous," and was soon followed by a. companion work devoted exclusively to women, under the title of " La Nef des Folles," just as the first edition of the " Dance of Death," which was printed in France under the name of " La Danse Macabre," was as immediately followed by " La Danse Macabre des Femmes." Nevertheless, it does not appear probable that the term Macabre originated in Germany.   The supposition that the name of the German poet was Macabre is, indeed, far less probable than that he might have named the poem after St. Macarius, while neither hypothesis is borne out by the known facts of the case, for we do not find a single German version bearing the title of " Macabre," or " Macabrean," but simply that of the " Doden Dänze," or " Todten Taenze."   Was it, then, a French author who composed the poem? and, if so, was the title founded upon the name of St. Macarius, or derived from some other source ?   Van Prael suggested that Magbar and Magbarah* were Arabic names for a cemetery; and this is possibly a hint that may eventually lead to a more satisfactory explanation of the term than that founded on the name of St. Macarius, and there is collateral evidence of some weight that may be brought forward in support of this view.   It is well known that Nicholas Flamel, who lived in the last half of the 14th century, and who enjoyed the various reputation of author, merchant, alchemist, and astrologer, was also a munificent benefactor of

* The Bibliophile Jacob ridicules this derivation, and jocosely suggests in its stead *Abracadabra.*

entitled "Van drén Konygen," and "Van den doden Konigen, und van den levenden Konigen." There were also English versions of the legend, one of which is preserved among the Arundel manuscripts in the British Museum. This English version of the "Three Living and the Three Dead," in addition to the interest of the subject, is remarkable as affording a curious example of the English language in a transition state. For instance, in the rude illumination at the beginning three kings, who are represented as pursuing the exciting amusement of the chase in a pleasant wood, suddenly meet three skeletons, at the sight of which, being naturally struck with dismay, the first king is represented as saying,—

> Ich am afert, lo what ich se
> Me thinketh hit beth develes thre ;

to which the first skeleton replies,—

> Ich wes wel fair—such skelton be—
> For Godes love be wer by me ;

which, put into rather more modern form, would read,—

> I am afeard !—lo ! what d'I see ?
> Methinks that it be devils three ;

the response being,—

> I, once well fair, now skel(e)ton be ;
> For God's love, then, be warned by me.

The characters of this legend are often changed in the different versions ; sometimes they are a king, a queen, and a nobleman ; sometimes three noble youths in gaily-broidered suits, and bearing richly-adorned weapons, revelling, as hunters, in the luxuries and privileges of rank and wealth. There is a very early representation of this version of the "Three Living and the Three Dead " in the church at Brie, near Metz.

Orcagna's celebrated "Triumph of Death " in the Campo Santo, at Pisa, painted in the 14th century, may be called an Italianized version of this legend. The three principal figures are the three kings of the original legend, but they are accompanied by their mistresses, and St. Macarius himself takes the place of the three skeletons, showing to the living kings three open graves, in which lie the bodies of three dead kings. In another part of the composition Death is symbolized by a female figure furnished with bats' wings and claws, and bearing a scythe, with which she sweeps down popes, emperors, kings, and others of all classes.

Here, then, we already find an extension of the range of the legend of St. Macarius to all classes, as carried out more definitely and distinctly in the "Dance of Death," which no doubt owed much of its immediate and lasting popularity, as previously suggested, to its fearless carrying out, in a more modern and expressive form, of the well-known verses of Horace—

> Pallida mors æquo pulsat pede pauperum tabernas,
> Regumque turres.

The more Northern expansion of this subject, whether we consider it as a series of stanzas forming a poem entitled "The Dance of Death," or as

a mere extension of the legend of St. Macarius, or as an original and more extensive work of analogous character, to which new verses were added from time to time as fresh characters were introduced, is asserted to have been of German origin,—a conclusion arrived at from the fact that the French and Latin verses attached to the earliest printed editions of the " Dance of Death " are stated, in more than one of the short prefaces or titles attached to those works, to have been translated from the German. On the other hand, with a view to explain the meaning of the term "Macabre," under which the first editions of the " Dance of Death " were issued in France, a few observations of an apparently opposite tendency may be conveniently made in this place. Firstly, if a German author either extended the poem of St. Macarius, or composed another of analogous but more extensive character, it seems probable that he would, or might, have founded his title on the name of the original author, and have termed his work the Macarian or Machabrian Dance, as some writers on the subject have suggested ; and an allusion closely bordering upon that suggestion occurs in the celebrated La Vallière catalogue, in which a MS. " Dance of Death " is described, with the note, " On l'a dit composé par un nommé Macabre." That the spirit of German satire of the period did actually run in that direction, both poetically and pictorially, is proved by the works of Sebastian Brandt, whose " Ship of Fools," in which personifications of all the leading types of human folly are represented as embarked in the Ship of Life, is an allegory closely resembling, in many respects, the " Dance of Death," while its profuse illustrations are not very dissimilar in general spirit to those belonging to that subject. It is worthy of note, also, that the " Ship of Fools " was translated from the German into French as "La Nef des Fous," and was soon followed by a companion work devoted exclusively to women, under the title of " La Nef des Folles," just as the first edition of the " Dance of Death," which was printed in France under the name of " La Danse Macabre," was as immediately followed by " La Danse Macabre des Femmes." Nevertheless, it does not appear probable that the term Macabre originated in Germany. The supposition that the name of the German poet was Macabre is, indeed, far less probable than that he might have named the poem after St. Macarius, while neither hypothesis is borne out by the known facts of the case, for we do not find a single German version bearing the title of " Macabre," or " Macabrean," but simply that of the " Doden Dänze," or " Todten Taenze." Was it, then, a French author who composed the poem ? and, if so, was the title founded upon the name of St. Macarius, or derived from some other source ? Van Prael suggested that Magbar and Magbarah* were Arabic names for a cemetery; and this is possibly a hint that may eventually lead to a more satisfactory explanation of the term than that founded on the name of St. Macarius, and there is collateral evidence of some weight that may be brought forward in support of this view. It is well known that Nicholas Flamel, who lived in the last half of the 14th century, and who enjoyed the various reputation of author, merchant, alchemist, and astrologer, was also a munificent benefactor of

* The Bibliophile Jacob ridicules this derivation, and jocosely suggests in its stead *Abracadabra.*

entitled "Van drén Konygen," and "Van den doden Konigen, und van
den levenden Konigen." There were also English versions of the legend,
one of which is preserved among the Arundel manuscripts in the British
Museum. This English version of the "Three Living and the Three
Dead," in addition to the interest of the subject, is remarkable as affording
a curious example of the English language in a transition state. For
instance, in the rude illumination at the beginning three kings, who are
represented as pursuing the exciting amusement of the chase in a pleasant
wood, suddenly meet three skeletons, at the sight of which, being naturally
struck with dismay, the first king is represented as saying,—

> Ich am afert, lo what ich se
> Me thinketh hit beth develes thre ;

to which the first skeleton replies,—

> Ich wes wel fair—such skelton be—
> For Godes love be wer by me ;

which, put into rather more modern form, would read,—

> I am afeard !—lo ! what d'I see ?
> Methinks that it be devils three ;

the response being,—

> I, once well fair, now skel(e)ton be ;
> For God's love, then, be warned by me.

The characters of this legend are often changed in the different versions ;
sometimes they are a king, a queen, and a nobleman ; sometimes three
noble youths in gaily-broidered suits, and bearing richly-adorned weapons,
revelling, as hunters, in the luxuries and privileges of rank and wealth.
There is a very early representation of this version of the "Three Living
and the Three Dead" in the church at Brie, near Metz.

Orcagna's celebrated "Triumph of Death" in the Campo Santo, at Pisa,
painted in the 14th century, may be called an Italianized version of this
legend. The three principal figures are the three kings of the original legend,
but they are accompanied by their mistresses, and St. Macarius himself
takes the place of the three skeletons, showing to the living kings three open
graves, in which lie the bodies of three dead kings. In another part of the
composition Death is symbolized by a female figure furnished with bats'
wings and claws, and bearing a scythe, with which she sweeps down popes,
emperors, kings, and others of all classes.

Here, then, we already find an extension of the range of the legend of
St. Macarius to all classes, as carried out more definitely and distinctly
in the "Dance of Death," which no doubt owed much of its immediate
and lasting popularity, as previously suggested, to its fearless carrying out,
in a more modern and expressive form, of the well-known verses of Horace—

> Pallida mors æquo pulsat pede pauperum tabernas,
> Regumque turres.

The more Northern expansion of this subject, whether we consider it as
a series of stanzas forming a poem entitled "The Dance of Death," or as

a mere extension of the legend of St. Macarius, or as an original and
more extensive work of analogous character, to which new verses were added
from time to time as fresh characters were introduced, is asserted to have
been of German origin,—a conclusion arrived at from the fact that the
French and Latin verses attached to the earliest printed editions of the
" Dance of Death " are stated, in more than one of the short prefaces or
titles attached to those works, to have been translated from the German.
On the other hand, with a view to explain the meaning of the term
" Macabre," under which the first editions of the " Dance of Death " were
issued in France, a few observations of an apparently opposite tendency
may be conveniently made in this place.   Firstly, if a German author
either extended the poem of St. Macarius, or composed another of analogous but more extensive character, it seems probable that he would, or
might, have founded his title on the name of the original author, and have
termed his work the Macarian or Machabrian Dance, as some writers
on the subject have suggested ; and an allusion closely bordering upon that
suggestion occurs in the celebrated La Vallière catalogue, in which a
MS. " Dance of Death " is described, with the note, " On l'a dit composé
par un nommé Macabre."   That the spirit of German satire of the period
did actually run in that direction, both poetically and pictorially, is proved
by the works of Sebastian Brandt, whose " Ship of Fools," in which personifications of all the leading types of human folly are represented as
embarked in the Ship of Life, is an allegory closely resembling, in many
respects, the " Dance of Death," while its profuse illustrations are not
very dissimilar in general spirit to those belonging to that subject.   It is
worthy of note, also, that the " Ship of Fools " was translated from
the German into French as "La Nef des Fous," and was soon followed
by a. companion work devoted exclusively to women, under the title of
" La Nef des Folles," just as the first edition of the " Dance of Death,"
which was printed in France under the name of "La Danse Macabre,"
was as immediately followed by "La Danse Macabre des Femmes."
Nevertheless, it does not appear probable that the term Macabre originated
in Germany.   The supposition that the name of the German poet was
Macabre is, indeed, far less probable than that he might have named the
poem after St. Macarius, while neither hypothesis is borne out by the
known facts of the case, for we do not find a single German version bearing
the title of " Macabre," or " Macabrean," but simply that of the " Doden
Dänze," or "Todten Taenze."   Was it, then, a French author who composed the poem? and, if so, was the title founded upon the name of
St. Macarius, or derived from some other source?   Van Prael suggested
that Magbar and Magbarah* were Arabic names for a cemetery; and this is
possibly a hint that may eventually lead to a more satisfactory explanation
of the term than that founded on the name of St. Macarius, and there is
collateral evidence of some weight that may be brought forward in support
of this view.   It is well known that Nicholas Flamel, who lived in the last
half of the 14th century, and who enjoyed the various reputation of author,
merchant, alchemist, and astrologer, was also a munificent benefactor of

* The Bibliophile Jacob ridicules this derivation, and jocosely suggests in its stead
Abracadabra.

entitled "Van drén Konygen," and "Van den doden Konigen, und van den levenden Konigen." There were also English versions of the legend, one of which is preserved among the Arundel manuscripts in the British Museum. This English version of the "Three Living and the Three Dead," in addition to the interest of the subject, is remarkable as affording a curious example of the English language in a transition state. For instance, in the rude illumination at the beginning three kings, who are represented as pursuing the exciting amusement of the chase in a pleasant wood, suddenly meet three skeletons, at the sight of which, being naturally struck with dismay, the first king is represented as saying,—

> Ich am afert, lo what ich se
> Me thinketh hit beth develes thre ;

to which the first skeleton replies,—

> Ich wes wel fair—such skelton be—
> For Godes love be wer by me ;

which, put into rather more modern form, would read,—

> I am afeard !—lo ! what d'I see ?
> Methinks that it be devils three ;

the response being,—

> I, once well fair, now skel(e)ton be ;
> For God's love, then, be warned by me.

The characters of this legend are often changed in the different versions ; sometimes they are a king, a queen, and a nobleman ; sometimes three noble youths in gaily-broidered suits, and bearing richly-adorned weapons, revelling, as hunters, in the luxuries and privileges of rank and wealth. There is a very early representation of this version of the "Three Living and the Three Dead" in the church at Brie, near Metz.

Orcagna's celebrated "Triumph of Death" in the Campo Santo, at Pisa, painted in the 14th century, may be called an Italianized version of this legend. The three principal figures are the three kings of the original legend, but they are accompanied by their mistresses, and St. Macarius himself takes the place of the three skeletons, showing to the living kings three open graves, in which lie the bodies of three dead kings. In another part of the composition Death is symbolized by a female figure furnished with bats' wings and claws, and bearing a scythe, with which she sweeps down popes, emperors, kings, and others of all classes.

Here, then, we already find an extension of the range of the legend of St. Macarius to all classes, as carried out more definitely and distinctly in the "Dance of Death," which no doubt owed much of its immediate and lasting popularity, as previously suggested, to its fearless carrying out, in a more modern and expressive form, of the well-known verses of Horace—

> Pallida mors æquo pulsat pede pauperum tabernas,
> Regumque turres.

The more Northern expansion of this subject, whether we consider it as a series of stanzas forming a poem entitled "The Dance of Death," or as

a mere extension of the legend of St. Macarius, or as an original and
more extensive work of analogous character, to which new verses were added
from time to time as fresh characters were introduced, is asserted to have
been of German origin,—a conclusion arrived at from the fact that the
French and Latin verses attached to the earliest printed editions of the
" Dance of Death " are stated, in more than one of the short prefaces or
titles attached to those works, to have been translated from the German.
On the other hand, with a view to explain the meaning of the term
" Macabre," under which the first editions of the " Dance of Death " were
issued in France, a few observations of an apparently opposite tendency
may be conveniently made in this place. Firstly, if a German author
either extended the poem of St. Macarius, or composed another of analogous but more extensive character, it seems probable that he would, or
might, have founded his title on the name of the original author, and have
termed his work the Macarian or Machabrian Dance, as some writers
on the subject have suggested; and an allusion closely bordering upon that
suggestion occurs in the celebrated La Vallière catalogue, in which a
MS. " Dance of Death " is described, with the note, " On l'a dit composé
par un nommé Macabre." That the spirit of German satire of the period
did actually run in that direction, both poetically and pictorially, is proved
by the works of Sebastian Brandt, whose " Ship of Fools," in which personifications of all the leading types of human folly are represented as
embarked in the Ship of Life, is an allegory closely resembling, in many
respects, the " Dance of Death," while its profuse illustrations are not
very dissimilar in general spirit to those belonging to that subject. It is
worthy of note, also, that the " Ship of Fools " was translated from
the German into French as " La Nef des Fous," and was soon followed
by a companion work devoted exclusively to women, under the title of
" La Nef des Folles," just as the first edition of the " Dance of Death,"
which was printed in France under the name of " La Danse Macabre,"
was as immediately followed by " La Danse Macabre des Femmes."
Nevertheless, it does not appear probable that the term Macabre originated
in Germany. The supposition that the name of the German poet was
Macabre is, indeed, far less probable than that he might have named the
poem after St. Macarius, while neither hypothesis is borne out by the
known facts of the case, for we do not find a single German version bearing
the title of " Macabre," or " Macabrean," but simply that of the " Doden
Dänze," or " Todten Taenze." Was it, then, a French author who composed the poem? and, if so, was the title founded upon the name of
St. Macarius, or derived from some other source? Van Prael suggested
that Magbar and Magbarah* were Arabic names for a cemetery; and this is
possibly a hint that may eventually lead to a more satisfactory explanation
of the term than that founded on the name of St. Macarius, and there is
collateral evidence of some weight that may be brought forward in support
of this view. It is well known that Nicholas Flamel, who lived in the last
half of the 14th century, and who enjoyed the various reputation of author,
merchant, alchemist, and astrologer, was also a munificent benefactor of

* The Bibliophile Jacob ridicules this derivation, and jocosely suggests in its stead
Abracadabra.

entitled "Van drén Konygen," and "Van den doden Konigen, und van den levenden Konigen." There were also English versions of the legend, one of which is preserved among the Arundel manuscripts in the British Museum. This English version of the "Three Living and the Three Dead," in addition to the interest of the subject, is remarkable as affording a curious example of the English language in a transition state. For instance, in the rude illumination at the beginning three kings, who are represented as pursuing the exciting amusement of the chase in a pleasant wood, suddenly meet three skeletons, at the sight of which, being naturally struck with dismay, the first king is represented as saying,—

> Ich am afert, lo what ich se
> Me thinketh hit beth develes thre ;

to which the first skeleton replies,—

> Ich wes wel fair—such skelton be—
> For Godes love be wer by me ;

which, put into rather more modern form, would read,—

> I am afeard !—lo ! what d'I see ?
> Methinks that it be devils three ;

the response being,—

> I, once well fair, now skel(e)ton be ;
> For God's love, then, be warned by me.

The characters of this legend are often changed in the different versions ; sometimes they are a king, a queen, and a nobleman ; sometimes three noble youths in gaily-broidered suits, and bearing richly-adorned weapons, revelling, as hunters, in the luxuries and privileges of rank and wealth. There is a very early representation of this version of the "Three Living and the Three Dead" in the church at Brie, near Metz.

Orcagna's celebrated "Triumph of Death" in the Campo Santo, at Pisa, painted in the 14th century, may be called an Italianized version of this legend. The three principal figures are the three kings of the original legend, but they are accompanied by their mistresses, and St. Macarius himself takes the place of the three skeletons, showing to the living kings three open graves, in which lie the bodies of three dead kings. In another part of the composition Death is symbolized by a female figure furnished with bats' wings and claws, and bearing a scythe, with which she sweeps down popes, emperors, kings, and others of all classes.

Here, then, we already find an extension of the range of the legend of St. Macarius to all classes, as carried out more definitely and distinctly in the "Dance of Death," which no doubt owed much of its immediate and lasting popularity, as previously suggested, to its fearless carrying out, in a more modern and expressive form, of the well-known verses of Horace—

> Pallida mors æquo pulsat pede pauperum tabernas,
> Regumque turres.

The more Northern expansion of this subject, whether we consider it as a series of stanzas forming a poem entitled "The Dance of Death," or as

a mere extension of the legend of St. Macarius, or as an original and more extensive work of analogous character, to which new verses were added from time to time as fresh characters were introduced, is asserted to have been of German origin,—a conclusion arrived at from the fact that the French and Latin verses attached to the earliest printed editions of the "Dance of Death" are stated, in more than one of the short prefaces or titles attached to those works, to have been translated from the German. On the other hand, with a view to explain the meaning of the term "Macabre," under which the first editions of the "Dance of Death" were issued in France, a few observations of an apparently opposite tendency may be conveniently made in this place. Firstly, if a German author either extended the poem of St. Macarius, or composed another of analogous but more extensive character, it seems probable that he would, or might, have founded his title on the name of the original author, and have termed his work the Macarian or Machabrian Dance, as some writers on the subject have suggested ; and an allusion closely bordering upon that suggestion occurs in the celebrated La Vallière catalogue, in which a MS. "Dance of Death" is described, with the note, "On l'a dit composé par un nommé Macabre." That the spirit of German satire of the period did actually run in that direction, both poetically and pictorially, is proved by the works of Sebastian Brandt, whose "Ship of Fools," in which personifications of all the leading types of human folly are represented as embarked in the Ship of Life, is an allegory closely resembling, in many respects, the "Dance of Death," while its profuse illustrations are not very dissimilar in general spirit to those belonging to that subject. It is worthy of note, also, that the "Ship of Fools" was translated from the German into French as "La Nef des Fous," and was soon followed by a. companion work devoted exclusively to women, under the title of "La Nef des Folles," just as the first edition of the "Dance of Death," which was printed in France under the name of "La Danse Macabre," was as immediately followed by "La Danse Macabre des Femmes." Nevertheless, it does not appear probable that the term Macabre originated in Germany. The supposition that the name of the German poet was Macabre is, indeed, far less probable than that he might have named the poem after St. Macarius, while neither hypothesis is borne out by the known facts of the case, for we do not find a single German version bearing the title of "Macabre," or "Macabrean," but simply that of the "Doden Dänze," or "Todten Taenze." Was it, then, a French author who composed the poem? and, if so, was the title founded upon the name of St. Macarius, or derived from some other source ? Van Prael suggested that Magbar and Magbarah* were Arabic names for a cemetery; and this is possibly a hint that may eventually lead to a more satisfactory explanation of the term than that founded on the name of St. Macarius, and there is collateral evidence of some weight that may be brought forward in support of this view. It is well known that Nicholas Flamel, who lived in the last half of the 14th century, and who enjoyed the various reputation of author, merchant, alchemist, and astrologer, was also a munificent benefactor of

* The Bibliophile Jacob ridicules this derivation, and jocosely suggests in its stead *Abracadabra.*

entitled "Van drén Konygen," and "Van den doden Konigen, und van den levenden Konigen." There were also English versions of the legend, one of which is preserved among the Arundel manuscripts in the British Museum. This English version of the "Three Living and the Three Dead," in addition to the interest of the subject, is remarkable as affording a curious example of the English language in a transition state. For instance, in the rude illumination at the beginning three kings, who are represented as pursuing the exciting amusement of the chase in a pleasant wood, suddenly meet three skeletons, at the sight of which, being naturally struck with dismay, the first king is represented as saying,—

> Ich am afert, lo what ich se
> Me thinketh hit beth develes thre ;

to which the first skeleton replies,—

> Ich wes wel fair—such skelton be—
> For Godes love be wer by me ;

which, put into rather more modern form, would read,—

> I am afeard !—lo ! what d'I see?
> Methinks that it be devils three ;

the response being,—

> I, once well fair, now skel(e)ton be ;
> For God's love, then, be warned by me.

The characters of this legend are often changed in the different versions ; sometimes they are a king, a queen, and a nobleman ; sometimes three noble youths in gaily-broidered suits, and bearing richly-adorned weapons, revelling, as hunters, in the luxuries and privileges of rank and wealth. There is a very early representation of this version of the " Three Living and the Three Dead " in the church at Brie, near Metz.

Orcagna's celebrated " Triumph of Death " in the Campo Santo, at Pisa, painted in the 14th century, may be called an Italianized version of this legend. The three principal figures are the three kings of the original legend, but they are accompanied by their mistresses, and St. Macarius himself takes the place of the three skeletons, showing to the living kings three open graves, in which lie the bodies of three dead kings. In another part of the composition Death is symbolized by a female figure furnished with bats' wings and claws, and bearing a scythe, with which she sweeps down popes, emperors, kings, and others of all classes.

Here, then, we already find an extension of the range of the legend of St. Macarius to all classes, as carried out more definitely and distinctly in the "Dance of Death," which no doubt owed much of its immediate and lasting popularity, as previously suggested, to its fearless carrying out, in a more modern and expressive form, of the well-known verses of Horace—

> Pallida mors æquo pulsat pede pauperum tabernas,
> Regumque turres.

The more Northern expansion of this subject, whether we consider it as a series of stanzas forming a poem entitled " The Dance of Death," or as

a mere extension of the legend of St. Macarius, or as an original and
more extensive work of analogous character, to which new verses were added
from time to time as fresh characters were introduced, is asserted to have
been of German origin,—a conclusion arrived at from the fact that the
French and Latin verses attached to the earliest printed editions of the
" Dance of Death " are stated, in more than one of the short prefaces or
titles attached to those works, to have been translated from the German.
On the other hand, with a view to explain the meaning of the term
" Macabre," under which the first editions of the " Dance of Death " were
issued in France, a few observations of an apparently opposite tendency
may be conveniently made in this place. Firstly, if a German author
either extended the poem of St. Macarius, or composed another of analogous but more extensive character, it seems probable that he would, or
might, have founded his title on the name of the original author, and have
termed his work the Macarian or Machabrian Dance, as some writers
on the subject have suggested ; and an allusion closely bordering upon that
suggestion occurs in the celebrated La Vallière catalogue, in which a
MS. " Dance of Death " is described, with the note, " On l'a dit composé
par un nommé Macabre." That the spirit of German satire of the period
did actually run in that direction, both poetically and pictorially, is proved
by the works of Sebastian Brandt, whose " Ship of Fools," in which personifications of all the leading types of human folly are represented as
embarked in the Ship of Life, is an allegory closely resembling, in many
respects, the " Dance of Death," while its profuse illustrations are not
very dissimilar in general spirit to those belonging to that subject. It is
worthy of note, also, that the " Ship of Fools " was translated from
the German into French as " La Nef des Fous," and was soon followed
by a companion work devoted exclusively to women, under the title of
" La Nef des Folles," just as the first edition of the " Dance of Death,"
which was printed in France under the name of " La Danse Macabre,"
was as immediately followed by " La Danse Macabre des Femmes."
Nevertheless, it does not appear probable that the term Macabre originated
in Germany. The supposition that the name of the German poet was
Macabre is, indeed, far less probable than that he might have named the
poem after St. Macarius, while neither hypothesis is borne out by the
known facts of the case, for we do not find a single German version bearing
the title of " Macabre," or " Macabrean," but simply that of the " Doden
Dänze," or " Todten Taenze." Was it, then, a French author who composed the poem? and, if so, was the title founded upon the name of
St. Macarius, or derived from some other source? Van Prael suggested
that Magbar and Magbarah* were Arabic names for a cemetery; and this is
possibly a hint that may eventually lead to a more satisfactory explanation
of the term than that founded on the name of St. Macarius, and there is
collateral evidence of some weight that may be brought forward in support
of this view. It is well known that Nicholas Flamel, who lived in the last
half of the 14th century, and who enjoyed the various reputation of author,
merchant, alchemist, and astrologer, was also a munificent benefactor of

* The Bibliophile Jacob ridicules this derivation, and jocosely suggests in its stead
Abracadabra.

HANS HOLBEIN'S

CELEBRATED

DANCE OF DEATH,

Illustrated by a Series of

PHOTO-LITHOGRAPHIC FACSIMILES

FROM THE COPY OF THE FIRST EDITION NOW IN THE
BRITISH MUSEUM.

ACCOMPANIED BY

EXPLANATORY DESCRIPTIONS

AND

*A Concise History of the Origin and Subsequent
Development of the Subject.*

BY

H. NOEL HUMPHREYS,

AUTHOR OF "A HISTORY OF THE ORIGIN OF THE ART OF PRINTING," OF
"THE ILLUMINATED BOOKS OF THE MIDDLE AGES,"
ETC. ETC.

LONDON:

BERNARD QUARITCH, 15, PICCADILLY, W.

1868.

PREFACE.

HE modern copies hitherto published of Holbein's celebrated "Dance of Death," although the work of very clever imitative artists, are necessarily wanting in that extreme accuracy which, in the reproduction of well-known works of art, is so desirable. In all copies 'by hand,' the touch and manner of Holbein and his engraver unavoidably lose much of the peculiar fascination and quaintness belonging to the originals ; and it was that conviction which induced me to attempt a series of positive facsimiles by one of the unerring processes of which photography is the basis.

It also seemed to me that the devices would lose much by being separated from the texts and verses which, in the original volume, serve as a partial framework and running commentary, forming an almost necessary part of the device itself. I have, therefore, reproduced the entire page belonging to each device.

Opposite to each facsimile will be found translations of the Latin texts and old French verses, accompanied by a brief description of the device ; not omitting those less prominent details by which the artist has often contrived to impart additional point, and pungency of satire, to the composition.

In the Introduction, devoted to an inquiry into the probable origin of the "Dance of Death," and also in my concluding remarks on its treatment subsequent to the time of Holbein, I have not attempted to enter. upon any of those strictly technical details which belong to the subject when studied from a specially Bibliographical point of view, but have rather sought, as briefly as possible, to trace such an outline of the subject as I deemed calculated to interest the general reader.

H. N. H.

HANS HOLBEIN

"THE DANCE OF DEATH."

——o——

F all the subjects, moral, religious, or allegorical, which have been profusely illustrated by the arts of the middle ages, no single theme has given rise to so striking a series of pictorial devices as that of the "Dance of Death." This curious and interesting series of semi-realistic, semi-symbolical compositions was gradually developed by several generations of mediæval artists, until it culminated, in the beginning of the 16th century, in those striking emblematic designs, generally attributed to Hans Holbein, which, in fertility of invention and power of artistic execution, have never, in their own peculiar vein, been surpassed, or even equalled, by any similar series, either ancient or modern. The subject was, in short, a most suggestive one, being at once a terrible, though at the same time grotesque satire, in which the incongruous combination of dancing and dying comprised a profound and philosophical criticism, and a sarcastically biting raillery upon the ordinary courses of human life in its various ranks.

It has been termed by a celebrated French critic a gallery of sublime buffoonery, a sepulchral phantasmagoria;* and by another French writer, "l'épopée lugubre;"—terms which are at once happily and accurately conceived; for the grim and sardonic crudity of the allusions, combined with an irresistible, though mocking and caustic drollery, are so intermingled with deeply tragic elements, often treated with a singularly poetical sense of grandeur, that the buffoonery itself seems to culminate in a kind of wildly horrible sublimity. Emile Souvestre, in his "Voyage à Basle," says, speaking of the "Dance of Death" originally executed there, more than a century before the time of Holbein, "On ne scaurait imaginer sans l'avoir vu, combien le peintre a dépensé de l'imagination pour varier et donner à chaque scène de la drame uniforme l'intérêt et l'imprévue de l'œuvre le plus varié." Baron Taylor and M. Jubinal express equal surprise at the energy and variety with which the subject has been treated; and Coxe, in his letters on Switzerland, expressed his unfeigned astonishment at the variety and invention displayed in the "Dance of Death" which he saw on the walls of the Dominican cemetery at Basle; while the art often displayed is

* M. Paul De la Croix (le Bibliophile Jacob).

of so high a kind that M. Fortoul does not hesitate to say of the woodcuts of the early printed editions of the subject that they vividly recall the style, at once large and delicate, of the painted glass of the 14th century, and are fit to rivalize with the very best specimens of the old schools of art of either Cologne or Florence. No other subject seized upon by the artists of the mediæval periods or those of the Renaissance has, in short, been so fruitful of striking results. Neither the "Ars Moriendi," with its groups of angels and demons contending for the souls of the departing, nor the "Ship of Fools," with its quaint and even savage onslaught upon all the vices and follies of the times, nor even the more genially satirical humours of "Renard the Fox," have led to such remarkable artistic results in the treatment of the respective series of illustrations to which they have given rise as the "Dance of Death." The same may be said of "La Danse des Aveugles," by Pierre Michault,* whose remarkable allegory of the three blind guides, Love, Fortune, and Death, with the appended moral, in which it is shown that, although a few may avoid the dominion of the two first, that of the last is inevitable, was almost as popular as the "Dance of Death." Yet neither did that work, though apparently so suggestive of artistic illustration, serve to develope any very remarkable series of designs. Nor did the three striking legends of "Cupido and Atropos," by Jean Lemaire, though some of the ideas are so picturesquely terrible, as, for instance, the one in which Cupid and Death accidentally meet in their rounds, and go to drink in a tavern, where, after their libations, they accidentally change weapons, Death taking the bow and shafts of Cupid, and Cupid the dart of Death. And it is to be remarked that, during the periods when these and other analogous subjects formed the favourite literature of Europe, the text of the author was often completely overlaid by the exuberance and abundance of the illustrative additions of the artist —a fact easily understood when it is recollected that the power of reading was confined to a few, while the capacity necessary to the understanding of a plainly and expressively drawn picture was possessed by all.

In order fully to appreciate the nature and peculiar merits of the "Dance of Death," whether as a poem, in its rude verses, or in the quaint symbolism of its pictorial illustrations, it is necessary to trace, as far as practicable, the origin of the idea, and the successive steps by which it appears to have attained its striking final development as a series of literary or pictorial devices intended to serve as a general *memento mori* to man and womankind of every state and station in life. That images of analogous character were in use in pagan times is well known, not only among the Greeks and Romans, but even with the Egyptians; and that a link of connection may be traced between the thoughts and customs of pagan times with those of the earlier Christian periods is tolerably evident. Herodotus informs us that the Egyptians placed a small image of a mummy upon the tables of their banquet-halls, as a reminder of the brief and uncertain duration of human life; and he also tells us that the Greeks adopted a similar symbol for the same purpose, a small model of an embalmed body being passed round to the guests at banquets, each guest in turn repeating the formula, "Eat, drink, and be merry, for when ye are dead ye will be like

* Who died in 1460.

this." The Greeks had also a far more poetical symbol, by means of which the immortality of the soul was expressed—that which forms the basis of the story of Cupid and Psyche, which may be briefly explained by reference to a well-known Greek gem,* engraved with the images of a skull and a butterfly, the one symbolizing death, the other immortality; the adoption of the butterfly as an emblem of the soul being, perhaps, one of the most graceful and poetical of all the semi-religious myths of Greek origin. Its application is, indeed, so obvious that it must be at once accepted as one of the most apposite symbols ever devised. It is evidently founded on the apparent death of the creeping larva or caterpillar, and its enclosure in the sarcophagus-like chrysalis, from which it eventually comes forth, furnished with beautiful wings, to enable it to soar into a higher sphere than that of its former existence. That this image (analogous to that of the scarabæus of the Egyptians) survived the pagan forms of civilization, and was still made use of in Christian times, is proved by the existence of several monuments, in which it is found introduced, most frequently in the form of a butterfly issuing from the mouth of a dying man, and so expressing the departure of the soul. This, then, may be considered a well-established link between the symbolism of the classical and modern periods—a connection acknowledged at a very early period by such writers as Eusebius, Gregory, and Clemens of Alexandria, who are found resorting to the philosophy and poetry of Greece for the pictures they have drawn of hell.

In the less poetic forms of Roman imagery, the suggestive image of the mummy-case and poetic symbolism of the skull and butterfly gave place to the human skeleton adopted as a *memento mori*, and this, perhaps, is the first step towards the building up of the master-work of mediæval allegory—the famous " Dance of Death." Petronius, in fact, when describing the banquet of Trimalcion, gives a somewhat detailed account of a small silver skeleton made to execute a series of dance postures by means of internal machinery, during which the host recited verses to the following effect:— "Alas ! alas ! how inconsiderate a thing is man ! A breath may puff away his fragile existence. We shall all be one day like this, when Pluto has seized his prey"—which is simply an Epicurean appeal inculcating the enjoyment of the present. A sarcophagus, sculptured with dancing skeletons, was discovered at Cumæ in 1810 ; and three dancing skeletons on an antique lamp, as described by Douce, were exhibited at a meeting of the Archæological Society of Rome in 1831—these images being intended to convey the idea that there was nothing really depressing or terrible in the passage from this life to a higher form of existence. But in these symbols there was no attempt to convey a terrible admonition concerning the special sins of various classes of society, accompanied by denunciations of future punishments, as in the mediæval " Dance of Death." Nevertheless, we find in them the root of the special kind of imagery which was developed with such powerful effect by the versifiers and artists of the middle ages. These pagan symbols are, in fact, as directly linked with mediæval imagery as are such Biblical figures as the skeletons evoked by Ezekiel, or as that of the " Angel of Death " who visited and destroyed

* Ficorni's " Gemmæ Literatæ," table vii.

the host of Sennacherib, as described in the passage so finely paraphrased by Byron,—

The Angel of Death spread his wings to the blast,
And breathed in the face of the foe as he pass'd.

M. Alfred Maury, in his paper entitled "Du Personnage de la Mort," informs us that after the captivity in Babylon the Jews confounded the Angel of Death with the Spirit of Evil, which they named Samael—formed of Hebrew words meaning *poison* and *God*—that is, God's poison. That blackness was associated with the aspect of personified Death we have an evidence in the "Alcestis" of Euripides, in which that character of the drama is described as "black-winged" or "black-robed," an idea which we shall eventually find associated with the "Dance of Death."

The dances which the Etruscans and other pagan nations connected with the rites devoted to the dead, and the spirit of which was in accordance with such images as those of dancing skeletons, were continued pretty far into the early Christian epochs, an instance of which may be cited from the "Manuel du Péché," usually ascribed to Bishop Grostete, and translated into English by Robert Mannynge (a Gilbertine canon). The instance in question is that of a party of dancers, who are described as meeting to dance in the churchyard of Cowek during the mass, after the custom had been for some time denounced by the clergy, as a relic of paganism, the officiating priest praying that they might dance for a twelvemonth without stopping— a prayer which was of course duly responded to. A similar event is described in the *Nuremberg Chronicle* as occurring in the reign of the Emperor Henry II.

These churchyard dances have, however, no direct connection with the series of verses and devices known as the "Dance of Death," except by association of ideas, and as exhibiting that strange mixture of the sacred and profane, in rites and ceremonies, as well as in works of art and litera- ture, which was one of the distinctive characters of the middle ages; works in which were blended a deep-seated religious superstition with an out- rageously burlesque and energetic humour; while both were united to that feeling of intensely earnest devotion which raised the vast cathedrals, and founded those magnificent monasteries still represented by structures which, in intricate richness of elaborate ornament, and even in bare dimensions, exceed the architectural monuments of any other age. Far more closely allied to the ideas developed in the "Dance of Death" were the Mysteries and Moralities, those curious dramas which supplied the place of the ancient theatre for a considerable period during the slow progress of modern civilization. All the records relating to these works have been perseveringly ransacked for allusions to the "Dance of Death" in the precise form in which we find it developed in the course of the 15th century, and not altogether without interesting results. The Mysteries, it is true, were, with more or less strictness, confined to the putting in action of well-known passages of the Scriptures, but in the "Moralities" which followed them, in which symbolic abstractions, such as Faith, Hope, Sin, and Death, were personified, we at once perceive the·creation of an acted drama of some- what similar tendency to the pictorial one of the "Dance of Death;" and of the more intimate connection of these dramatic performances with this subject I shall have further occasion to remark upon.

Another branch line of research has led some of our archæological investigators to consider the scourge of the great plagues of the 13th and 14th centuries as having suggested the idea of warning men of the uncertainty of life, by representing Death in the act of striking down all classes with indiscriminate alacrity; and, in fact, the desolating ravages of the pestilences in various parts of Europe may be figuratively described as rather like a reckless and horribly fantastic dance than the usual measured march of the destroyer.* M. Peignot, one of the most industrious, and at the same time fanciful investigators of all matters pertaining to mediæval archæology, has even put forward the ingenious suggestion that the plague of 1373 exhibited peculiar characteristics which may have had to do with the actual devices of the "Dance of Death," those who were struck by it being almost immediately seized with convulsions of an unusual kind, which resembled, though in a grotesque and horrible manner, the action of dancing, in the contortions of which the patients died. It may be admitted that the symptoms of this plague, thus categorically described, suggest a temptingly plausible theory to speculative archæologists; but in the face of other evidence of more probable character it cannot be seriously entertained.

It is time to turn to sources which appear to be more immediately connected with the origin of the celebrated "Dance of Death." In the 10th century, according to M. du Meril, appeared St. Fulbert's "Vision of Death," which may have contained the literary germs of the subject; but a far more direct source seems to have developed itself, about 1250, in the legend known in France as "Le dit des trois morts et des trois vifs," generally attributed to the Egyptian ascetic St. Macarius. Both these works obtained a very wide spread circulation, and, after a certain lugubrious fashion, became extremely popular. One of the causes of their favourable reception by the general masses of society, and quite independent of the undoubted religious enthusiasm which stirred the whole of Christendom at that period, was the simple fact that it set strikingly forth the perfect equality of both rich and poor in the face of Death, which, in an age when the social demarcations were of the most marked and impassable character, rendered even such a social leveller as Death a popular personage. The last-named legend has for its principal feature the unexpected meeting of three kings, or nobles, with three skeletons; and the dialogues which successively ensue between them take the form of a rude legendary poem. There are several French versions of this production, the best known being those of Baudouin de Condé and Nicholas de Marginal, both of which are striking and forcible in style from their crude simplicity. Manuscripts of these works are often accompanied by one or more illuminated illustrations, generally rather rude in character, but occasionally of considerable artistic merit,—the treatment of the three Deaths being precisely similar to that adopted in the earlier "Dances of Death." There were also many German versions, two of the best known being respectively

* In 1348 the Rhine country suffered such fearful ravages that in Strasbourg alone 1,600 were carried off within a very brief period, out of a comparatively small population.

entitled "Van drén Konygen," and "Van den doden Konigen, und van den levenden Konigen." There were also English versions of the legend, one of which is preserved among the Arundel manuscripts in the British Museum. This English version of the "Three Living and the Three Dead," in addition to the interest of the subject, is remarkable as affording a curious example of the English language in a transition state. For instance, in the rude illumination at the beginning three kings, who are represented as pursuing the exciting amusement of the chase in a pleasant wood, suddenly meet three skeletons, at the sight of which, being naturally struck with dismay, the first king is represented as saying,—

> Ich am afert, lo what ich se
> Me thinketh hit beth develes thre ;

to which the first skeleton replies,—

> Ich wes wel fair—such skelton be—
> For Godes love be wer by me ;

which, put into rather more modern form, would read,—

> I am afeard !—lo ! what d'I see?
> Methinks that it be devils three ;

the response being,—

> I, once well fair, now skel(e)ton be ;
> For God's love, then, be warned by me.

The characters of this legend are often changed in the different versions ; sometimes they are a king, a queen, and a nobleman ; sometimes three noble youths in gaily-broidered suits, and bearing richly-adorned weapons, revelling, as hunters, in the luxuries and privileges of rank and wealth. There is a very early representation of this version of the "Three Living and the Three Dead" in the church at Brie, near Metz.

Orcagna's celebrated "Triumph of Death" in the Campo Santo, at Pisa, painted in the 14th century, may be called an Italianized version of this legend. The three principal figures are the three kings of the original legend, but they are accompanied by their mistresses, and St. Macarius himself takes the place of the three skeletons, showing to the living kings three open graves, in which lie the bodies of three dead kings. In another part of the composition Death is symbolized by a female figure furnished with bats' wings and claws, and bearing a scythe, with which she sweeps down popes, emperors, kings, and others of all classes.

Here, then, we already find an extension of the range of the legend of St. Macarius to all classes, as carried out more definitely and distinctly in the "Dance of Death," which no doubt owed much of its immediate and lasting popularity, as previously suggested, to its fearless carrying out, in a more modern and expressive form, of the well-known verses of Horace—

> Pallida mors æquo pulsat pede pauperum tabernas,
> Regumque turres.

The more Northern expansion of this subject, whether we consider it as a series of stanzas forming a poem entitled "The Dance of Death," or as

a mere extension of the legend of St. Macarius, or as an original and
more extensive work of analogous character, to which new verses were added
from time to time as fresh characters were introduced, is asserted to have
been of German origin,—a conclusion arrived at from the fact that the
French and Latin verses attached to the earliest printed editions of the
"Dance of Death" are stated, in more than one of the short prefaces or
titles attached to those works, to have been translated from the German.
On the other hand, with a view to explain the meaning of the term
"Macabre," under which the first editions of the "Dance of Death" were
issued in France, a few observations of an apparently opposite tendency
may be conveniently made in this place. Firstly, if a German author
either extended the poem of St. Macarius, or composed another of analogous but more extensive character, it seems probable that he would, or
might, have founded his title on the name of the original author, and have
termed his work the Macarian or Machabrian Dance, as some writers
on the subject have suggested; and an allusion closely bordering upon that
suggestion occurs in the celebrated La Vallière catalogue, in which a
MS. "Dance of Death" is described, with the note, "On l'a dit composé
par un nommé Macabre." That the spirit of German satire of the period
did actually run in that direction, both poetically and pictorially, is proved
by the works of Sebastian Brandt, whose "Ship of Fools," in which personifications of all the leading types of human folly are represented as
embarked in the Ship of Life, is an allegory closely resembling, in many
respects, the "Dance of Death," while its profuse illustrations are not
very dissimilar in general spirit to those belonging to that subject. It is
worthy of note, also, that the "Ship of Fools" was translated from
the German into French as "La Nef des Fous," and was soon followed
by a companion work devoted exclusively to women, under the title of
"La Nef des Folles," just as the first edition of the "Dance of Death,"
which was printed in France under the name of "La Danse Macabre,"
was as immediately followed by "La Danse Macabre des Femmes."
Nevertheless, it does not appear probable that the term Macabre originated
in Germany. The supposition that the name of the German poet was
Macabre is, indeed, far less probable than that he might have named the
poem after St. Macarius, while neither hypothesis is borne out by the
known facts of the case, for we do not find a single German version bearing
the title of "Macabre," or "Macabrean," but simply that of the "Doden
Dänze," or "Todten Taenze." Was it, then, a French author who composed the poem? and, if so, was the title founded upon the name of
St. Macarius, or derived from some other source? Van Prael suggested
that Magbar and Magbarah* were Arabic names for a cemetery; and this is
possibly a hint that may eventually lead to a more satisfactory explanation
of the term than that founded on the name of St. Macarius, and there is
collateral evidence of some weight that may be brought forward in support
of this view. It is well known that Nicholas Flamel, who lived in the last
half of the 14th century, and who enjoyed the various reputation of author,
merchant, alchemist, and astrologer, was also a munificent benefactor of

* The Bibliophile Jacob ridicules this derivation, and jocosely suggests in its stead
Abracadabra.

religious institutions, and an active restorer and beautifier of sacred edifices. In the last-named character he made several additions to the entrance-gates of the Cemetery of the Innocents, adding an inscription in what has been termed hieroglyphics, but which it is far more probable was simply a series of Arabic characters, in which the Arabic name of a cemetery, *magbarah*, may possibly have been written.

This inscription in Oriental characters seems to point to the Eastern origin of some custom or name connected with cemeteries.   The transcription into Arabic letters, of a name or general inscription, which had possibly been in use long before Flamel's time, having possibly arisen from a kind of vanity of the learned astrologer, who wished to display his knowledge of Oriental literature, which was probably only a smattering picked up in his so-called studies connected with alchemy and the "black art," most of the treatises on those subjects being derived from the works of Oriental writers.   It is also on record that he embellished the renovated gateway with certain figures, which, in accordance with his hieroglyphic or Arabic inscription, he may have caused to be made as representations of negroes in Oriental costume, negro eunuchs being frequently employed as the guardians of Eastern cemeteries; or, the figure of a negro may have been thought by Flamel appropriate to the situation, as a mediæval version of the idea of the ancients, according to which figures either of Death or Sleep were painted black in pictorial compositions, and in sculpture were wrought in black marble, or some other material of that colour.   This view of the subject is further supported by the representations of the entrance-gate of a cemetery, which frequently occur in the early French editions of the "Danse *Macabre*," in which devices the figure of a negro in Oriental costume is represented as standing above the gate in the act of uttering the death call, and blowing a kind of rude horn by way of summons; the device of the negro being generally accompanied by verses, entitled the "Cris de Mort," which embodies a general summons to the inevitable final destiny of humanity.   This theory may, or may not, contain the true germ of an explanation of the term Macabre.   But, in support of the hypothesis, it may be urged that the French illustrated editions of " La Danse Macabre " were in some way directly founded on the painting at the Cemetery of the Innocents, which is proved by the presence in those editions of the subject entitled "Le Roy Mort," which certainly refers to Charles V., who, according to the old French writer Noel du Fail, caused the painting to be executed; while, in support of the view that the term existed before the time of Flamel's renovation of the gates of the Cemetery of the Innocents, it may be stated that one of his contemporaries, Jean le Febure, after an almost miraculous recovery from an attack of the plague, wrote a kind of thanksgiving poem, in which the line occurs—

Je fis de Macabre la Danse,

from which some have ventured to affirm that he was the author of the famous series of stanzas bearing that name; but the passage is evidently only an allusion to the "Dance of Death," which he had so nearly performed, and serves to show that it was known in France by the title of " Danse Macabre " as early as 1376, while none of the early German versions of the subject are known by that designation. It is to be noted also that the original work of the Egyptian ascetic Macarius may have contained allusions to Eastern cemeteries by their Arabic name, which allusions, instead of his own name, may have led to the partial adoption of the term in France.

The subject, whether developed out of the legend of the " Three Living and Three Dead," or from the Vision of St. Fulbert, or as an original but closely analogous production, had at an early epoch already assumed a permanent generic form, from which its subsequent variations were for a long period very inconsiderable. In poetry, in painting, and in sculpture, Death, under the form of a ghastly corpse rather than a skeleton, was represented as addressing himself in succession to persons of every rank and station, and inviting them (as a sovereign *invites*, by *command*) to join him in a *dance*, terminating in the pitfall of the grave ; in each case the grim humour of the invitation and the uselessly evasive character of the reply being wrought out, whether in the verses or the devices, with wonderful point and variety, and always conveying more or less of the rough popular notions of justice. The curate, for instance, is reproached with his petty exactions, the cardinal with his idle luxury, while, in the Basle version, the fat abbot is brutally told that he has prepared himself to rot quicker than his fellows ; while the Jew and the miser are both overwhelmed with stinging sarcasm, and the doctor fares no better with the grim satire of Death than he did with that of Rabelais and Molière. But his summons is always tempered to the poor, the suffering, and the aged. He leads off the cripple along with the rich man, saying, in the Basle version,—

> Der Tod aber wil sein Freund syn
> Er nemmt ihn mit dem Reichen hin.

In some of the Continental versions the victims are ready with bribes and promises to Death if he will but let them go. On an Italian device, for instance, of Death and the Poor Man, the latter, who has nothing to give, exclaims,—

> All my goods I'll freely give
> If thou wilt but let me live.
>
> (Tutto ti voglio dare,
> Se mi lasci scapare.)

And sentences of similar import occur in many of the verses of the German editions.

The first well-authenticated example of a mural " Dance of Death " with a date is that which was executed in 1312 on the walls of a convent situated in a suburb of Basle called the Klingenthal, on the lower shore of the Rhine, opposite the main portion of the city. The painting occupied near seventy yards of one of the walls of an interior gallery, a corridor of the convent, and was first noticed by a baker of artistic proclivities named Buschel, who succeeded in making an accurate and very interesting copy of the whole series of subjects ; and his work is preserved in a volume now in the library of the University of Basle (marked B. 111, 8 (2). It is supposed that the original painting served as the model upon which the superior work in the upper city was founded a century and a half later. The date of the Klingenthal painting was clearly traceable at the time the copy was taken by Buschel, and was annexed to the device representing Death and the Baron, being expressed as follows :—"*Dussent Jor drei hundert und* xij." (a thousand years, three hundred and xii). On the suppression of the convent, the buildings in the Klingenthal became a salt-warehouse, and the original paintings have entirely disappeared.

The next example is that in the church at Minden, a composition not precisely in the usual form, as the figures are represented dancing in a ring, which appears to support the theory which supposes that the "Dance of Death" had its direct origin in the churchyard dancing previously alluded to, or in the fanatical religious dances of a sect which had many followers at that period. Fabricius assigns the date 1380 to this work.

The next example, and one of the most important and interesting, as being mentioned in contemporary records, is that which has always been known by the now celebrated name of "La Danse Macabre," and which was executed by an anonymous artist at the gate of the cemetery of the Innocents, in Paris, most probably on the walls of the adjoining cloister, as stated by Stowe when describing the "Dance of Death" in old St. Paul's. It appears to have been sculptured in relief, and painted. The contemporary record principally alluded to occurs in a journal kept during the reign of Charles VI. of France, and is to the following effect :—"Item l'an 1424 fut faite la Danse Macratre [for Macabre] aux Innocents ; el fut commencée environ le moys d'Aoust et achevé au carême suivant." M. Barante, the historian of the Dukes of Burgundy, and also M. Villarets, in the face of this precise statement, appear to consider (relying upon another record of the period) that the "Danse Macabre" was an acted performance instead of a polychrome sculpture; and perhaps they were right, notwithstanding the contemporary record just cited ; for M. Branche, in a report of the *séances de la Société pour la Conservation des Monuments* (Caen, 1842), asserts that, æsthetically speaking, the "Danse des Morts" was both *danced* and *painted*, such performances (founded originally, perhaps, on the funereal and other ritualistic dances previously alluded to) being of the same character as the "Mysteries" and "Moralities," in which there were spoken dialogues between Death and his victims, similar to those of the poems. M. Kestner is of this opinion, and gives examples from funereal carols in support of it. The actors of Death were naked, says M. Branche, with the exception of a few shreds of red cloth, repulsively intended to represent falling portions of decaying flesh ; and he cites a miniature in a MS. preserved in the Bibliothèque Impériale, in which an acted "Dance of Death" is represented with the figures dressed in this manner. He states also that the actors discoloured their skin, and crimped their hair so as to look like that of a negro, which seems to afford some sort of clue to the figure of the negro or black man, found in the early French editions of the "Danse Macabre." M. Kestner quotes a passage from a book of accounts, in which the actual payment to some monks, as performers of a dramatic representation of the "Dance of Death," is set forth—the remuneration consisting in certain barrels of wine, and other refectorial condiments.

The next examples are those at Strasbourg, and in one of the churches in

Dijon ; after which the subject became very popular as a church decoration in many parts of France and Germany. But the "Dance of Death," as a mural decoration, which at an early period was the most celebrated, was certainly the one executed about the year 1441, by an anonymous artist, upon the walls of the Dominican cemetery close to one of the gates of the city of Basle, the main characteristics of which were evidently copied from the painting in the suburb of the Klingenthal, with the addition, possibly for the first time, of direct personal allusions,—a feature which was one of the principal causes of the immediate and lasting popularity of that work, while its erroneous attribution in recent times to the pencil of Holbein has greatly tended to continue its celebrity. The execution of this painting was possibly suggested by the ravages of the great epidemic of 1438, which carried off so many victims during the protracted sittings of the well-known Council which met on the 21st of July, 1431, and continued its labours till 1449.

The best and earliest account of this work is that published by the engraver Merian in 1649, who asserts that all the figures were actual portraits of contemporary personages, citing as very conspicuous, and beyond doubt, those of Pope Felix V., the Emperor Sigismund, Albert King of the Romans, and others who were present at the Council of Basle.

The order in which the subjects occurred cannot now be ascertained, as the remains of the work, after several restorations* by more or less unskilful hands, were some years ago detached from the wall, to save them from total decay, and placed in the crypt of the cathedral, without much attention to the order of the few subjects which remain intact. It may be mentioned here that in Merian's plates of this work the first feature, and that, too, made a very important one, is not found in the other "Dances of Death" of the 15th century. This feature consists of a preacher addressing words of warning to a congregation composed of persons of every rank ; while further on is seen a charnel-house filled with human skulls and bones, from which two figures of Death are issuing, playing on a kind of flageolet and tambourine. This device was afterwards retained, with additions and improvements, in all the versions of the subject founded directly on the Basilean series. It has been said that the treatment of the figure of Death in two of Holbein's designs was immediately founded on two of those of the Basle series ; but if that be the case, the great artist did not avail himself of either of the two most striking of that series, that in which Death has a skull strapped round his waist in guise of a drum, while he uses a shin-bone as a drumstick, as he leads off his Holiness the Pope, or that in which Death arrests a miser in the act of weighing his gold as he walks along a country road. There is every reason to believe that the subject with the preacher was added by the painter Hans Klauber, when he repaired the work in 1568, after the Reformation, more than a century after the execution of the original devices. This is rendered the more probable by the figure of the

---

* It was retouched by Klauber in 1568, and again in 1616 and 1621 by another hand ; after which it was copied by Merian. It was entirely painted over in 1703, and finally repaired in 1805. This is the series which has been so frequently attributed to Holbein, though originally painted a century before his time.

Preacher, which is a portrait of Œcolampadius, one of the most ardent advocates of the Protestant doctrines. Among other mural "Dances of Death" which have been alluded to by modern writers on the subject, was one in the cloister of the cathedral at Amiens, known as the "Danse Macabre," the last remains of which were recklessly obliterated so recently as 1817. There was also a "Dance of Death" in the church of St. Maclou at Rouen; while at Fecamp the same subject was sculptured upon the columns. The "Dance of Death" at Strasbourg, previously alluded to, bears the date 1450, and was possibly the work of Martin Schœn. At Berne, Nicholas Emmanuel Deutch painted a "Dance of Death" on the walls of the cemetery in 1484; while others are described as having been executed at Lucerne, at Lubeck, at Dresden, and several other places. Among the few examples of frescoes of the "Dance of Death" which still remain sufficiently perfect to convey a tolerably correct idea of their original characters, that one recently brought under notice in the Temple Neuf at Strasbourg deserves especial mention, as also the one discovered in the church of Chaise Dieu in Auvergne, of which an account, with copious illustrations, was published in 1841 by M. Achille Jubinal. There is also one in the church of Clusone, near Brescia, in the north of Italy, of which M. Vallardi of Milan published an account in 1859. This last, a work of the middle of the 15th century, is a very important composition, forming one grand picture, which might be compared without disadvantage to the best works of Giotto or Filippo Lippi. The Italian antiquary Zandetti, writing in 1845, described another Italian "Dance of Death," then recently brought into notice at Como. The subject does not, however, appear to have taken such firm hold on the popular taste in Italy or Spain, as in France, Germany, and England.

Before quitting the subject of the mural illustrations of the "Dance of Death," it should be remarked that in the earlier examples the treatment varied very considerably, and it was not till after the middle of the 15th century that a finally settled form and order appears to have been adopted; for instance, in the Lubeck Dodendantz, the hour-glass, a classical symbol, is freely introduced, while in the painting in the Temple Neuf at Strasbourg that symbol is nowhere used; and a still more remarkable distinction is to be noticed in the painting at Lubeck, in which the figure of Death is represented as armed with a sword, and riding on a lion as an emblem of destruction, going about, as it were, "like a roaring lion, seeking whom he may devour."

I have no intention of even briefly alluding to all the monumental examples which have been referred to by recent writers, and more or less copiously described and illustrated, as such a list would be out of place in a short preface; but it is well to allude to their existence, *en passant*, as showing the great interest which this singular series of devices has excited among modern archæologists.

The illustrations of the "Dance of Death" which occur in the MSS. are of nearly, if not quite equal, antiquity with the mural paintings just described. M. Champollion Figeac alludes to an illuminated MS. of the 15th century, formerly in the library of the Château of Blois. Others, also, have been noticed, especially the following, cited by M. Kestner, who remarks that among other versions of this subject occurring in MSS., either in the text only or accompanied by illustrations, the following may · be noted. First, there are German MSS. with different versions of the text, of 1443 and 1449, in the Royal Library of Munich, and two others at Heidelberg, as described by Massmann. In most instances these German versions, like the series of German devices, are accompanied by an introductory sermon addressed to Pope ——, and at the end a second discourse (*dy ander Predig*). One MSS. has also a third, reviewing the whole series of the ordinary common-places usually set forth concerning the uncertainty of life. In the illustrations, the Preacher and his assistants are almost invariably figures of Death. Among other MSS. containing the "Dance of Death," cited by M. Kestner as being in the Bibliothèque Impériale at Paris, some contain only the verses without any illustration ; and in one of these the " Doctor " is called Machaber, whether merely as a stroke of satire it is difficult to determine. One of the MSS. thus cited is illustrated with very finely wrought miniatures, and has the same verses as the early-printed French editions, and was probably executed about the same time. A MS. in the Escurial, said to be much earlier, is assigned to the 14th century, and is called " La Danza general de Muerte," &c. ; but the title accords so closely with that of the French-printed editions, with the exception of the omission of the word Macabre, that the work looks more like one of the 15th century than the 14th. One of the most remarkable instances in which this subject is introduced in a MS. executed in the first half of the 15th century, occurs in a volume now before me, the property of William Bragge, Esq., of Shirle Hill, near Sheffield, who has kindly allowed me to carry it away for a time from the shelves of his library, which abounds in bibliographical treasures of great interest and curiosity. In Mr. Bragge's MS. the usual series of devices is connected by a light scroll-work of richly-coloured foliage, in the adroitly-artistic manner peculiar to the illuminators of the period, so as to form ornamental borderings to the two first pages of the Service for the Dead, to which they form enrichments of a more than usually elaborate and appropriate character. The armorial bearings upon a shield attached to one of the first illuminations of this MS. appear to suggest that it was executed for a Duke of Burgundy (?), or an immediate connection of that ducal family, and was probably, judging from the figures of a bride and bridegroom in the principal border, a wedding present. These two figures appear, indeed, to be those of a duke and duchess of Burgundy, who are accosted by a grim figure of Death. Immediately below them is a king addressed in a similar manner,—evidently, by the robe embroidered with fleurs-de-lis, a king of France ; while below are a ,pope and an emperor, the latter evidently the Emperor of Germany ; and from about this period the king and the emperor are nearly always represented by a king of France and an emperor of Germany. The Death which seizes the Pope carries a coffin, as in most of the more recent devices, though, in some cases, it is exchanged for a mattock or a grave-digger's spade. The devices of this particular class are cleverly adapted to the forms of the borders in which they are introduced,—a child snatched by Death from its cradle forming the subject of the narrow border of the top. These devices are superior in general artistic merit to those of the first printed books, which they preceded by perhaps more than half a century. They are also better than most of the frescoes, of which I have seen good fac-similes, except the Italian one of Clusone; and in point of high finish and graceful treatment they are superior to any other versions of the subject previous to that which emanated from the genius of Holbein.

Before proceeding to describe the first examples of the "Dance of Death" in the form of printed books, as they occur in the successive editions in which the subject gradually assumed the forms which culminated in the matchless designs attributed to Holbein, it will not be without interest to allude, very briefly, to what is known regarding the pictorial illustration of the "Dance of Death" in England, previously to the time of Holbein. Felibien, the celebrated French archæologist and architect, who in the reign of Louis XIV. collected so many interesting particulars connected with the history of art in the middle ages, has stated, incidentally, in his "History of the Antiquities of Paris," that the idea of the "Dance of Death" *originated* in England; but those who have cited his statement to that effect have not observed that he is evidently alluding to the church-yard dances, and not to the actual poem or its illustrations. Nevertheless, it is now ascertained that the subject became at an early period of its development as popular in England as on the Continent. Sir Thomas More, for instance, speaks of the "Daunce of Death pictured in Paules;" and Stowe, in his "Antiquities of London," has given a somewhat detailed account of it. It appears that "John Carpenter, town-clerk of London in the reign of Henry VI., caused, with great expense, to be painted upon board, about the north cloister of St. Paul's, a monument of Death leading all estates, with the speeches of Death, and the answer of every state;" and these paintings appear to have remained intact till they were removed, after the Reformation, by order of the Protector Somerset. In another place, Stowe speaks of the subjects in question as the "Dance of Macha-bray," and says it was like the one painted about the Innocents' cloister at Paris. The "metres or poesies," that is to say the descriptive verses appended in the continental versions to each of the subjects, were trans-lated into English by the poet John Lydgate, and have been preserved complete—though, unfortunately, without the illustrations—in Tottel's edition of the "Fall of Princes."* The order of arrangement seems to have been nearly the same as that of the first printed copy of the "Danse Macabre" published in Paris in 1485 by Guy Marchant, as will be seen in the description of that book.

In many of the early versions of the "Dances of Death," after the example started at Basle, portraits of well-known characters were introduced by way of giving extra piquancy to the devices, an interesting example of which occurs in the St. Paul's series, in which a portrait of Rekyll, the royal juggler, or tregetour, in the reign of Henry V., whose effigy was introduced, accompanied by a special set of verses, in which Death addresses him in the usual fashion,

* Dugdale, also, in his "History of St. Paul's," gives an account of this series of paintings.

alluding whimsically to his calling; to which Rekyll is made to reply as follows:—

> Lygardemayne now helpeth me right nought;
> Farewell my craft, and all such sapience,
> For Deth hath more maistries than I have wrought.

The painting in St. Paul's was far from being the only English example of the "Dance of Death." Older than that at St. Paul's was the one in the Hungerford chapel at Salisbury, traces of which have been recently discovered; while at Stratford-on-Avon there appears to have been a series of the "Dance of Death" which must have been well known to Shakespeare, who, possibly, was equally well acquainted with the engraved series attributed to Holbein. It is probable, indeed, that either the one or the other may have suggested to him the idea of "Death's book,"* in "Measure for Measure;" and also the lines in "Richard II.," act 3, scene 2—

> Within the hollow of a crown
> That rounds the mortal temples of a king
> Keeps Death his court; and there *the antic* sits,
> Scoffing his state, and grinning at his pomp.

"There the antic sits" would really seem to refer very directly to the grotesque attitude of the grinning skeleton, who sits behind the Emperor in the Holbein series, in the act of discrowning him.

As another example of English versions of the "Dance of Death," I may mention the tapestry worked with that subject in the Tower, which is referred to in an inventory of the property belonging to King Henry VIII., under the title of the "Dance Macabre;" and I may also call attention to the beautifully-sculptured series of the usual devices of the subject which still exist in the decorations of the oak stalls of St. Michael's, Coventry.

The first appearance of the "Dance of Death" in print was in the rude form of the "block-books," in which both the illustrative devices and the text were engraved upon blocks of wood of the size of the entire page, each page of the work, whether composed of a simple device, or a device combined with text, or of text without a device, being printed from a single block of wood on which an entire page of the matter, illustrative or descriptive, was engraved. The application of wood-engraving to the production of cheap books in the form described appears to have come into use about the beginning of the 15th century; and the subject of the "Dance of Death" having attained great popularity at that time, it is somewhat surprising that it did not form one of the first and most frequently-treated subjects of the engravers of block-books; the more especially as its extent was precisely suited to the narrow capacities of that class of volume.† But so far from this being the case, I only know of two examples, both excessively rude in design and execution. In the first of these, which I examined in the Royal Library at Munich, which is unusually rich in its collection of block-books,—the order of the subjects

* Quoted by Mr. Douce, with a number of other interesting particulars.
† The earliest class of block-books seldom exceeded twenty or thirty leaves in bulk.

is, in the main, that which is found in the late printed versions, the first
being the Death-summons of the Pope, the second that of the Emperor, the
third that of the Cardinal, the fourth that of the King, &c.   The treatment,
however, is different, in many respects, from that more generally adopted,
the figure of Death not being always in the usual dancing attitude ; for
instance, in addressing the Pope he has taken his seat by the side of the
papal throne, and quietly strikes up the tune of his fatal dance on the
bagpipe.   This mode of proceeding is perhaps intended as a kind of
deference to the exalted rank of the Pope, then deemed the first among
the princes of the earth, and who is therefore granted a few moments of
preparation ; for in most of the other subjects the victim is at once
actively clutched by a dancing Death.   The cuts in this small volume are
rudely coloured, and accompanied by German verses roughly written by
hand on the opposite page.   Judging from the somewhat primitive artistic
treatment of this series of devices, I should feel inclined to assign it to a
very early date, the more especially as the character of the designs does not
appear to have as yet fallen into the regular conventional form which they
eventually assumed.   The mere fact of excessive rudeness of execution, it
may be asserted, is no guide whatever as to date, inferior artists having
executed block-books of the very rudest kind at a period when the art had
attained to its greatest perfection.   But other characteristics of this production also suggest an early date ; and it is not without interest to note that
the style of the devices, especially in the repulsive features of the snake-
like creatures which are twined about and eating through the flesh of the
figures of Death, very closely resemble those of the earliest known edition
with the text printed from moveable types, namely, the " Doden Dantz,"
in the library of Strasbourg.

The only other specimen of a block-book " Dance of Death " which I
have seen is the one preserved at Heidelberg, in which the whole
series is as coarsely executed as the Munich specimen, while the conception is far less repulsive, and the style of art purer and in every way
superior.   Each subject is accompanied by German verses placed above
the device in which Death announces his challenges to the fatal dance, the
reply of the doomed victim being placed below.   This block-book, with
its accompanying verses, both devices and text, being of entirely German
character, would serve to add somewhat to the evidence in favour of the
German origin of the " Dance of Death," either with or without illustrations ; and it is to be observed, that there were other German versions
which have not come down to us, as the German verses attached to the
devices of the work under description are evidently not those from which
Desreys made his Latin translation for the versions afterwards published in
France, though of the same import.   My supplemental plate (No. 1) of
" Death and the Knight," the twelfth device of this series, will convey
a fair general idea of the treatment of the other subjects ; it is half the size
of the original.   The armour of the knight serves to fix the date of this
work as that of the first half of the 15th century.

We now come to the books of the " Dance of Death " printed with
moveable types in the newly-invented " Printing Press "—that greatest
result of the mental activity and progress of the stirring 15th century.   It

appears somewhat extraordinary that very few German versions of the "Dance of Death," and those uncertain as to date, appear to have issued from the German printing-press, between the time of its *début* in Mayence, with Gutenberg's magnificent Bible in 1455, and the first establishment of the printing-press in Paris in 1470, especially as the German presses had greatly multiplied during that period, and works of almost every class had been issued. According to Massmann, however, exceedingly early editions of the " Dance of Death " *did* issue from the German presses. This learned bibliophilist actually assigns one undated edition to 1459, and another to 1470 ; but these assumed dates are of a highly speculative character, and the first edition to which an approximate date can be assigned with any degree of probability, is that discovered in the public library of Strasbourg by M. Jung, in 1852, which is attributed to the year 1480, a date to which both Panzer and Fiorillo assign German editions of the " Todten Tantz." It has been most minutely described by M. Kestner in his recent work. The illustrations of that volume are, as previously stated, in the style of those of the Munich block-book, and equally repulsive, though very superior in point of execution. The book is a small folio, said to be printed at Strasbourg, then a city within the limits of the German empire, and is entitled " Die Doten Danz, mit figuren," &c. &c. As far as we know at present, this appears to be the first authentic edition of this singular work ever produced by the printing-press ; and it is worthy of remark that this, as well as other early German editions, is simply styled the " Dance of Death," with no allusion to the term Macabre, which may turn out to belong only to those versions of which the illustrations are founded, on the original French paintings at the Innocents', as previously suggested. Should the supposed date of 1480 prove correct, the Strasbourg volume may be the very edition from which Guy Marchant used the verses for his French edition, and from which Desreys afterwards made his Latin translation from the German, as stated in the title to one of the earliest of the editions of the " Danse Macabre." The " Dance of Death " is followed in this rare volume by the dialogues of the " Three Dead and Three Living " and a few other pieces. The next German editions at present known are those of Lubeck, dated respectively 1496 and 1510, both bearing the same title as the Strasbourg volume, both being subsequent to the earliest French editions.

The earliest edition of the " Dance of Death " printed in France was, as just stated, that issued by Guy Marchant in 1485, entitled, as we have seen, " La Danse Macabre," &c. &c. It was a small folio volume, with the illustrations neatly executed in outline, with less vigour than the German devices of the Strasbourg volume, but also without their more repulsive adjuncts. The first illustration to this edition is a cut representing the author at his desk, in the usual style in which that subject was treated in the 15th century, whether in MSS. or in printed books. Beneath the device is the author's address to his readers, in doggrel verse, which I give below, together with a free translation :—

O creature roysonnable, Qui desire vie éternelle, Tu a cy doctrine notable Pour bien finir vie mortelle.	O reasoning ones, of human kind, If ye would earn eternal life, The doctrines herein ye may find To finish well this mortal strife.

These verses, as well as all those which refer to the individual subjects, forming additions to the original legend of the "Three Dead and the Three Living."

In the next illustration we find two skeletons represented, each furnished with a different kind of musical instrument, upon which they appear to be playing the grim tunes to which their victims will be compelled to dance. This is a feature much enlarged upon in the subsequent treatment of the subject by more advanced artists, until the group of victims of the introductory illustration eventually became known as the "Orchestra of Death," and it is sometimes termed the "Triumph of Death," the scene being transformed into a grand processional march, in which victims of all ranks are following the music of Death to their doom. The growth of this device is curious. One of the block-book editions I have noticed is altogether without it, while in Guy Marchant's first edition, now under description, we find only two figures, as in the mural devices, while in the Strasbourg edition of 1480 four had already appeared. Beneath the two figures of Death are their respective addresses (which seem like mere amplifications of those belonging to the legend of the "Three Living and the Three Dead"), the first of which is reproduced below, with a free English translation :—

Vous par divine sentence	All men, by a divine decree,
Qui vivés en estatz divers,	Who live in high or low estate,
Tous, danserez ceste danse	Must dance this dance along with me
Une fois et bons, &c.	To their inevitable fate.

These passages appear to show very clearly that the idea of such a series of devices was, as in the original legend, simply a form of warning to prepare for death ; and it may be remarked also that, far from the figures of the victims themselves being made to exhibit those contortions which were the fatal symptoms of the "Dancing Plague" of the 13th century, the rudely drawn figures in this series appear stolidly inactive, as though paralyzed by the suddenness of the fatal summons ; while Death, on the other hand, cuts merry capers as he drags each new partner into the fated dance. It is, therefore, not so much a dance of the victims as literally that of Death himself, triumphing in his work, that was represented, both by the name and the devices of this singular painted drama, which is so peculiarly characteristic both of the tone of thought and also of the special direction taken by art in the 13th, 14th, and 15th centuries.

The series of subjects in Guy Marchant's "Danse Macabre" is ordered with a scrupulous regard to the conventional arrangements of society, regarding the rights of priority which belonged to different social conditions from the highest to the lowest ; and though Death in almost every subject invariably announces himself in the text as a non-respecter of state or station, the artist and the author have not felt themselves in the same independent position in the marshalling of their personages ; but have felt compelled to the punctilious observances of well-trained heralds, or accomplished masters of the ceremonies. Consequently, before even emperors or kings, comes the Pope, to whom Death assigns the first place, as he thus addresses him in verses which I have translated as follows :—

Dam, Pape, vous commencerés,
Comme le plus digne seigneur,
En ce point honoré serés,
Aux grans maistre est deu l'honneur.

So, Pope, come lead the dance with me;
A potent signor such as you
In this, at least, must honoured be,
For to the great is honour due.

His Holiness does not appear to appreciate this delicate attention as he
ought to do, and exclaims,—

Hée! faut il que la danse mainne
Le premier? Qui suis Dieu en terre,
J'ai eu dignité souverainne
En l'Eglise, comme Saint-Pierre? &c.

What! I lead off the dance with thee?
I—God on earth—be thus compelled?
I? holding that high sovereignty
That once the sainted Peter held?
What! seized on thus, like any other?
Why not have taken some poor brother?

It is in this fashion that Death invites one after another to his dance,
and that his partners in turn reply, each acknowledging in turn that
resistance is useless. In the order of the devices the Emperor, habited as
the Emperor of Germany, follows the Pope, but the King does not come
next. After the Emperor, in those days of ecclesiastical supremacy, comes
the Cardinal—the second dignitary of the Church taking precedence of the
second in rank among temporal princes. In the same spirit of carefully
studied arrangement, the Legate precedes the Duke. In the marshalling
of the professions and trades, however, down to the minstrel, the jailer,
and the agricultural labourer, no especial order is observed.

The French verses of the first editions published in France have been,
curiously enough, attributed by no less an authority than Warton to
Michel Marot, the son of the celebrated Clement Marot, the translator of
the Psalms of David into French verse,—a supposition which is singularly
erroneous, inasmuch as Clement Marot himself was not born till 1495,
ten years after the appearance of Marchant's edition of the "Danse
Macabre." It is, however, possible that they were translations from the
German by Jean Marot, the first of this family of poets, who may possibly
have written them, as he flourished at the precise time, and is known to
have composed verses of that kind, while the defects of the verses in question
precisely agree with those signalized by French critics as disfiguring the
poetical productions of the first of the Marots. By whomsoever these
verses may have been written, they frequently possess not only much
cleverly-turned satire, but also display occasional flashes of genuine
poetry; so much so, in fact, that M. Kestner conceived the idea of setting a
selection of them to music in the form of a cantata not altogether dissimilar in
plan to Mendelssohn's "Walpurgis Night;" and with this view, he secured
the services of M. Edouard Thierry to recast them in the mould of modern
verse, which that gifted writer has done with the zest of true genius, some
passages of this new version of the "Epopée Lugubre" being exceedingly
beautiful, as the following example of his remodelling of the dialogue
between Death and the Child may serve to show, even in the paraphrased
translation which I have appended :—

L'ENFANT.

Mes petits pieds sont comme ceux des anges,
Ma mère avec amour
Ote et remet l'épingle de mes langes,
Pour les voir tout le jour.

THE CHILD TO DEATH.

Like angels' feet, my little feet
As yet have never touched the ground;
My mother's kisses, long and sweet,
Upon my tiny toes abound.

Sur ses genoux (pauvre tête blonde)
Je fais à peine un pas......;
Comment veux tu que j'entre dans ta Ronde,
Moi qui ne marche pas.

She on her lap, with loving glance,
Tempts my first step with coaxing talk;
Then say, how can I join thy dance
Before I yet have learned to walk?

LE MORT.

Quand vos petits pieds sont si frêles,
Enfant, je vous prêterais des ailes;
En place donc, pour commencer,
Pas de replique—il faut danser.

DEATH TO THE CHILD.

Thy little feet are useless things,
But I, my child, will lend thee wings.
So take thy place—fall in, fall in,
The dance is going to begin.

Another edition appeared in 1486, to which was added, for the first
time, a special "Danse Macabre des Femmes." This volume is also of
extreme rarity. It is entitled "La Grande Danse Macabre des Hommes
et des Femmes, avec les dits des trois morts et trois vifs, le debat du corps
et de l'ame, la complainte de l'ame damnée et l'enseigment pour bien vivre
et bien mourir." The title of "La *Grande* Danse" denotes of course a
further extension of the subject, which is, in fact, directly alluded to in the
epilogue or colophon as follows :—" Here ends the illustrated 'Dance of
Macabre,' augmented by several new personages and fine axioms,"—" *Cy finit
la Danse Macabre, historiée et augmentée de plusieurs nouveaux personnages et
beaux dits.*" The supposed connection between the "Legend of St.
Macarius" and the "Danse Macabre" is, as some have thought, strongly
supported by the introduction of the hermit with his discourse, supposed by
some to be intended for St. Macarius himself, but who may rather be
the French Saint Fulbert, sometimes spelt Philibert, who wrote an essay
similar to that found attached to the device of the hermit in the French
editions of "La Danse Macabre." Soon after the appearance of the
edition of 1485, Verard is supposed to have issued his folio version, of
which there is a rudely-coloured copy in the Bibliothèque Impériale. A
smaller edition of about the same period is also attributed to Verard, of
which there is a very finely illuminated copy in the Bibliothèque Impériale,
printed on vellum on one side only, the devices being so exquisitely coloured
and illuminated that they rival the miniatures of the finest MSS. In 1490
a Latin edition was issued by Godfrey de Marnef, at the sign of The Peli-
can, in the Rue St. Jacques, with his name and printer's mark attached,
the text being translated from the German into Latin, as stated in the title,
by Peter Desreys. In the subsequent editions of Desreys' version the
allusion to the German original is in the following words :—" Versibus
Allemanicis (id est, in morem ac modos rithmorum Germanicorum com-
positis)," from which it might be inferred that it was the metre of the
German verses rather than their matter that had been adopted. This is a
large quarto edition, the figures of which are very superior to those in the
editions of Guy Marchant. The subjects are in pairs, something after
the manner of those in the celebrated " Speculum Humanæ Salvationis,"
surrounded by a framework or canopy of architectural character. The Pope,
in this edition, is led off by a Death, who with his right arm supports a
coffin ; the Emperor being evidently intended, as in the edition of 1485,
for the Emperor of Germany, as indicated by the double-headed eagles on
his robe ; while the King is as evidently the King of France.

It was either this edition, or the fine Lyons quarto of 1494, which served as the model for the fully equal, if not superior, work published at Troyes by Nicholas le Rouge in 1528. The Lyons edition of 1494 just alluded to, which bears no publisher's name, is a very remarkable work, the plate representing the figures of negroes at the gate of the cemetery being, as in the Marnef and Le Rouge editions just alluded to, conspicuous features, while the supplemental subjects of Death and the printers, and Death and the bookseller, are very interesting. Although a later production than the Marnef edition, the framework of the subject is Gothic, as shown in the annexed supplemental plate (2), while that of the Marnef edition is in the style of the Renaissauce. In 1492 appeared the edition of Gillet Coustian, a copy of which was sold in 1862 in La Salle Silvestre for 1,170 francs ; and in 1500, Nicholas de la Barre, at the sign of the Arms of France, in the Rue de la Harpe, published a very rude version of the "Danse Macabre," with illustrations in the style of those of Guy Marchant. In this poor edition several of the devices are repeated, and made to do duty three or four times over ; for instance, the figure of the astrologer serves also as that of the schoolmaster. This edition contains also "The Three Dead and the Three Living." There is a copy of it in the British Museum, from which several of the devices were engraved in facsimile by Samuel and Richard Bentley, who published twenty-five copies on vellum and twenty-five on paper, one of the first named of which I have recently examined in Mr. Bragge's library, and found the style of the original well preserved.

Before the treatment of the subject by Holbein, other French editions appeared in rapid succession, of which the following may be named :— Guyot's "Danse Macabre des Femmes, &c., augmentée de nouveaux personnages,"—Paris, 1491 ; "La Grande Danse Macabre des Hommes et des Femmes,"—Lyons, 1499 ; "Danse Macabre des Hommes et des Femmes," &c.—Nicholas Rouge, Troyes, 1500 (?), and another, without date, by Jean Garnier, of the same place ; another, by Guilleaume de la Mane, Rouen, 1500 (?) ; and by Nourry, Lyons, 1501 ; at Geneva, 1503 ; Le Rouge, Troyes, 1531 ; and by Denys Janot, Paris, 1533. But it would be altogether unprofitable in a brief essay of this kind to attempt to give a complete list of all the editions, which neither Fiorillo, in his learned article " Ueber die Todentanze," nor Brunet, in his more recent list, nor even M. Massmann and M. Kestner, the latest authorities on the subject, have as yet succeeded in doing. It may be well to note, however, that previously to the entirely original treatment of the subject by Holbein, several versions of the German series, under the generic title of the "Todten Dantz" (variously spelt) had appeared, among which the Lubeck editions of 1496 and 1520 are especially mentioned by M. Massmann, and also that the " Grande Danse Macabre" was frequently copied, in an extremely rude manner, especially by Nicholas Rouge and Jehan Lecocq, of Troyes, who, after issuing some fine editions, appear to have made a special trade of preparing cheap books of the kind for the periodical fairs, which were very inferior to most of the other versions. The blocks of one of these rude Troyes editions are still in existence, and have been recently discovered and used to print a modern edition by M. Horneman, of Lille. I have to remark also in this place that it is not possible to pass over without note the treatment of this favourite subject in the borders of the printed books of "Hours," for which the printing-presses of Paris became so celebrated soon after the time of the first issues of the "Danse Macabre." "The first appearance of these subjects in the borders," says Langlois, following Massmann, "was in 1491;" but this is an error, for I have now before me a beautiful "Book of Hours," on vellum, executed by Pigouchet for Simon Vostre, which bears the date 1488, a page from which forms my third supplemental plate. The subjects from the "Dance of Death," as introduced in the "Horæ," were generally worked into little compartments in the decorative borders, either with or without accompanying couplets to point the moral. They appeared first in the "Hours" published by Simon Vostre; and their effective and highly-finished execution, considering their miniature dimensions, is often quite extraordinary. The annexed specimen will convey a favourable idea of the artistic cleverness of these effective little compositions, which are perfect marvels of the arts of the engraver and designer at that early epoch. They have not, however, the artistic freedom, nor the profusion of symbolic enrichment, which was very soon afterwards destined to be infused into the subject. The advance which the arts of designing and engraving achieved during the first ten or twelve years of the 16th century was, indeed, so marvellous and so rapid, that it seems more like an artistic bound than a steady advance; it was, as it were, a sudden dash of progress, stimulated in the highest degree by the striking genius of a galaxy of great and original artists who appeared in Germany at that epoch, the greatest among whom was Hans Holbein, and his great contemporaries Albert Durer and Lucas Cranach.

Taking into consideration this rapid artistic movement, it is easy to conceive that the treatment of such a subject as the "Dance of Death" would be likely to present striking evidences of that advance, presenting, as it does, a field for artistic imagination and execution such as scarcely any other series of subjects could furnish. It afforded, indeed, those rare opportunities for the mingling of the serious and the humorous, of the tragic and the comic, which, perhaps, no other subjects in the form of a series could offer. The highest kind of mediæval art had not, however, been brought to bear upon this series of subjects till the pencil of Hans Holbein was engaged to treat them. It is principally upon the strength of the devices about to be described in this work that Holbein is supposed to have painted a "Dance of Death" at Basle—either at the Town-house or elsewhere. Sandraart, in his "Life of Rubens," tells us that that celebrated artist often declared he had derived great advantage from studying the compositions of Holbein's "Dance of Death," and critics have too hastily jumped to the conclusion that, as there was a celebrated "Dance of Death" at Basle, and as Holbein was by birth a Basilean, he must necessarily be the author of it; thus arriving at the erroneous conclusion that a "Dance of Death" at Basle, by Holbein, was necessarily the one alluded to by Sandraart. If, however, Sandraart's work be examined a little more thoroughly, we shall find that, while describing a remarkable portrait of Henry VIII. by Holbein, in the palace of Whitehall, he goes on to say that there is another work in that building which constitutes that painter the very Apelles of his art; and Mr. Douce was of opinion that a "Dance of Death" was possibly alluded to. This conjecture is strengthened by the fact that the poet Prior does actually speak of a "Dance of Death" by Holbein in the ode on the death of the Duke of Buckingham :—

> Imperious Death directs the ebon lance,
> Peoples great Harry's tomb, and leads up Holbein's Dance.

If the conjecture respecting a "Dance of Death," painted by Holbein while in England, be well founded, then the passage referring to the admiration of Rubens is explained, for, although it is very uncertain whether that great painter ever stayed at Basle for any length of time, there is no doubt about his having resided for many months in London, or, that during his stay he painted the ceiling of the banqueting chamber in the new part of the palace of Whitehall, and he may there have seen the "Death's Dance" by Holbein, which has been described as of life size, and which Sandraart would seem to say placed its author in the position of a very Apelles of his art. It is true that he, as well as Prior, may possibly allude to the well-known series of engravings attributed to the pencil of Holbein, the more particularly as the author of the lines at the end of that volume compares the artist to Zeuxis, while Sandraart, not to follow too closely a previous writer, may possibly have made the comparison with Apelles; but there is much evidence in favour of a painted series on the walls of Whitehall.

With regard to the question whether Holbein ever executed a "Dance of Death" on a large scale at Basle, it should not be forgotten that Bishop Burnet, in his "Travels in Switzerland" (and the Bishop was well acquainted with matters pertaining to art), distinctly alludes to a "Dance of Death" at Basle, painted on the "walls of a house" by Holbein, adding that the paintings in question were nearly obliterated, while those of the same subject at the Dominicans' had been recently repainted. Patin also speaks of a series of paintings on a house at Basle, but does not mention the subject. But whether or not Holbein executed a series of frescoes or oil-paintings of the "Dance of Death" either in London or in Basle, there is pretty good evidence that he was engaged in other ways upon that favourite subject as early as 1530, having been employed to adapt it to the enrichment of a dagger and sheath, the devices of which are the "Dance of Death," while M. Fortoul cites a picture attributed to him, in which the great artist's peculiar aptitude for analogous subjects is illustrated with singular force and ingenuity. In this work a young girl is represented playing on a sort of guitar, while a mysterious magician holds a looking-glass before her, in which are dis-

sidered their author ; in explanation of which criticism it may be observed
that Holbein's style had very little of the usual Germanic mannerism, and
that he has, in fact, been styled the German Raphael. There is every
reason to believe that this celebrated alphabet, with the "Dance of
Death," was designed by him for the Basilian printers Bebelius and
Cratander, as it appears first in works issuing from their press. These
alphabets, which are thought by some to be actually superior in general artistic
merit, and especially in humour, to the series of the larger subjects, were
certainly executed at Basle, where a proof impression of the whole on one
sheet may still be seen. They were most probably engraved on metal, as
appears by the excessive sharpness of the work, which was undoubtedly that
of Hans Lützenberger form-schneider-in Basel, as signed by the engraver
himself. This exquisite series of initials, of which two distinct sets were made,
one less than the other, were soon used by many other printers, as well as
those of Basle, and were several times copied. An ingenious French critic has
thought he perceived, on a careful examination of this series of letters, that
the subject of the design within each letter was invariably one the name of
which commenced with the letter which it served to decorate—as, for
instance, the M has the Medicus (physician), the N the Numericus (the
banker), the P the Præliator (soldier), &c. But many of the other subjects
do not fit so well, and the idea can only be considered in the light of an
ingenious fancy.

But while there is abundant evidence of the authorship of these
alphabets, there is no positively direct proof which enables us to assign to
Holbein the far more important and almost matchless series of designs for
the illustrations to the "Dance of Death," published at Lyons in 1538
under the title of "Les Simulacres et Faces Historiées de la Mort," &c.,
and yet such is the internal evidence afforded by the work itself that no
careful student of art can feel a moment's doubt upon the subject.
Borbonius, the friend and contemporary of Holbein, has, indeed, left some
epigrammatic lines in his "Nugæ" which appear to leave no doubt that he
considered his great artist-friend the author of the work in question. The
verses, with their title, are—

DE MORTE PICTA A HANSO PICTORE NOBILI.

Dum mortis Hansus pictor imaginem exprimit,	Death again lives by Holbein's skill,
Tanta arte mortem retulit, ut mors vivere,	And breathing quits the tomb's dark portal;
Videatur ipsa—et ipse se immortalibus	And, by the glory of his art,
Parem diis fecerit, operis hujus gloria.	The painter, too, is made immortal.

Other evidence also exists to show that even at the time of their execution
these cuts were generally acknowledged to be the work of Holbein ; for
instance, the four first subjects, relating to the Creation and Fall of man,
were used by the same Lyonese publishers in their series of Scripture
subjects, which have never been doubted as the work of Holbein, and afterwards, when the same four subjects were reproduced in England as illustrations in Cranmer's Catechism, the name of Hans Holbein as that of
the designer was attached to them at full length. That this continued to be
the conviction is corroborated by similar evidence about a century later, on

the publication of the copies by Hollar in 1647, to which were appended a monogram and initial, ⊦B. i., intended to express "Hans Holbein invenit," as proved by the words in full, which occur in one or two places. The attribution of the work to Holbein had, indeed, been made without hesitation long before the time of Hollar, and has been with as little doubt reasserted since.

The famous version of the "Dance of Death" now under description, published in Lyons in 1538 by Gaspar and Melchior Treschel, when that city had become one of the most celebrated centres of the early achievements of the printing-press, was in every respect superior, both in conception and execution, to all the previous editions.* The devices were not composed in illustration of the original quatrains of the old "Danse Macabre," but of a series of passages from the Old and New Testaments, the texts appearing above the device, in the Latin of the Vulgate, and a free metrical translation in the shape of a quatrain underneath the picture ; the latter being possibly composed by Gilles Corrozet, while the author of a Latin version of these lines was Georgius Æmilius, the brother-in-law of Luther. Notwithstanding the genuine stamp of Holbein's style which this series of devices displays, the claim set up for him as the artist-producer has been hotly disputed, as previously stated, and it is certainly true that his name nowhere appears upon the plates of the original editions, although it was very usual with him to sign his works. It is also well known that in some verses attached to the work, composed in honour of the artist or artists of the illustrations, other names than those of Holbein are mentioned. The publisher, also, at the time of publication (1538), expresses his regret for the death of the artist who had designed such elegant figures, while it is known that Holbein was living in England nearly twenty years after that date,—a difficulty not easy to explain away ; yet when we proceed to examine the dedication "to the Abbess Jeanne de Touzelle, of the Convent of St. Peter at Lyons," of whose existence no satisfactory evidence can be found, the suspicion of a wilful mystery becomes very strong ; and the next point to be considered is, whether there was any necessity for mystification of that kind.

The directly personal as well as satirical nature of some of the designs at once suggests a sufficient clue to the desirability of concealing their authorship. It is true that the nature of the satire is only of that form which had developed itself in some of the very earliest versions of the "Legend of St. Macarius," such as introducing the features of well-known sovereigns and princes as those of the victims. But times had altered ; sovereigns were become more sensitive and more despotic, while the hits administered in this last version were more pointed, personal, and political than heretofore. There

---

* Some bibliographers have supposed that this series of cuts had already appeared at Basle, probably as early as 1530, either in the form of a sheet or as a book ; in support of which a proof-sheet is cited, with German verses above and below, which has been assigned to that date. But if works of such excellence had ever been published, either as a sheet or a book, it is difficult to conceive that not a single copy should have been preserved. The first public appearance of the work at Lyons in 1538 may, however, have occurred in consequence of the brothers Treschel having first become acquainted with them at the time they were engraving Holbein's drawings for the "Historiarum Veterum Instrumenti," etc., in which case the Lyonese artists cannot be considered as the engravers of them, as I have suggested in another place.

is especially an attempt to elevate the character of the Imperial court at the expense of that of France. For instance, in the device of the Emperor (which, as usual, is the Emperor of Germany), Maximilian I. is evidently represented, and he is seen in the act of administering justice ; while in the device of the King (as usual, the French King), Francis I. is as evidently intended, and his royal pursuits are indicated as being more especially those of the banquet table and its associated dissipations, from which he is about to be summoned by the skeleton, who fills to him a bowl of wine of truly regal magnitude.* Analogous distinctions are made between the Empress and Queen, and there are other strokes of direct and biting satire equally likely to bring down regal vengeance from a sovereign who had banished the illustrious printer, Robert Estienne, from the soil of France under the pressure of priestly bigotry.

These, then, are sufficient reasons, it should seem, why the authorship of these pasquinades of the pencil should have been concealed, and the best mode of concealment was stating that the artist was dead. I shall therefore assume that, with two exceptions, these designs are the genuine work of Hans Holbein, the stamp of whose peculiar genius and manner they indubitably bear ; for surely, if any other artist of the time had possessed the genius to execute them, his name would not have remained utterly unknown to posterity. This new version of the " Dance of Death," now generally admitted to be a Holbein version, though not quite so extensive as to the number of devices relating to the main subject, is yet far more complete in its general scope than any of the preceding ones. We are, indeed, made to begin at the beginning, and are introduced to man before his disobedience subjected him to the dominion of his inevitable destroyer. The first device of the Holbein series represents the Creation, and more especially the creation of Eve, as one of the instruments of the temptation, which led to the doom of death ; the second subject being the scene of the actual temptation. The third is the Expulsion, when Death first appears in the background ; and the fourth, Adam condemned to till the earth, with Death at his side. Next comes Holbein's amplification of the Basle subject of two Deaths leaving the charnel-house, and with which the edition of 1542 commences, omitting the four first devices. This subject, as treated by Holbein, has been termed the "Orchestra of Death ; " and it may be observed here that so various are the musical instruments introduced into this funereal orchestra that M. Kestner has published a special work upon the subject, in which he enumerates and describes eighteen distinct kinds. After "Death's Orchestra," sometimes called the "Triumph of Death," as transformed into a procession in later forms of treatment, comes the first subject of the actual series which consists of thirty-four successive devices representing Death in the act of summoning to his dance men of every social grade. Then follows a composition representing the Last Judgment, and then a symbolical tail-piece. Only thirty-four devices, it is seen, are devoted to the actual series, including both men and women, while in the early editions of Guy Marchant there are forty subjects in the " Danse Macabre des Hommes," without counting those of the "Danse

---

* In the Cologne edition of this version, published after the death of Francis, the portrait of Henry II. is substituted.

Macabre des Femmes," which in the "*Grande Danse* Macabre" were published as a separate series in the same volume. But the judicious selection of the most characteristic subjects, and the fertility of invention and artistic power with which they have been enriched and generally treated, more than compensate for the absence of some of the less suggestive subjects of the older editions.

It has been observed that Holbein has, in two instances, copied the attitude of his figure of Death from the Basle series,—the first in plate 11, where Death appears as a jester, and the second in plate 35, where he is beating the drum before the newly-married couple. But these figures in the Basle paintings may, on the contrary, have been copied from Holbein at the time of some of the restorations; and even if Holbein's devices be really taken from those at Basle, his treatment is so superior as to make them his own; for it is to be especially observed that he entirely discarded the repulsive figure of the decaying body as impersonating the idea of Death, and adopted the perfect skeleton as his image, thus gaining in the direction of the picturesque at the same time that he abandoned the more gross and repulsive forms adopted by his mediæval predecessors. M. Kestner, in his excellent treatise, has erroneously stated that in the "Danses Macabres" Death is nearly always represented by a body entirely stripped of flesh—a true skeleton (au corps entièrement dépouillé de ses chairs, une véritable squelette); but this is not so, as proved by Guy Marchant's first edition, now before me, and the early editions issued at Lyons and Troyes. It was not, in fact, till Holbein treated the subject that the pure skeleton was introduced. The decaying body was the grosser image adopted by the artists of the middle ages; the skeleton, the more refined symbol devised by those of the Renaissance. In the early French books of (printed) "Hours" the frontispiece of the anatomical man was at first simply a repulsive dead body, like the mediæval image of Death; but in the later editions of the "Hours," issued by Simon Vostre in 1507, the figure is made a pure skeleton, showing the general art tendency of the period.

The first and the last subjects in Holbein's series--namely, the Creation and the Last Judgment—appear to present some differences of style, which render it possible that they may be the work of another hand. Are they, then, it may be asked, the work of the artist* who had commenced the illustration of the work before it was taken up by Holbein? If the first subject be carefully examined, it may perhaps suggest to the critic that, not-withstanding the general dexterity of the composition, it does not appear to possess that magisterial decision of outline and that sparkling crispness of

* Holbein's friend, Nicholas Borbonius, in a work published at Lyons in 1538, the year in which the "Dance of Death" appeared, under the title of "Les Simulacres et His-toriées Faces de la Mort," &c., praises two painters, Hans Ulbius (doubtless Holbein) and George Reperdius, as equal to Parrhasius and Zeuxis. It is possible that he may allude to both the designer and engraver of these wonderful devices; or may we not here have the clue to the allusion made by the publisher to the death of his artist, who may have been Reperdius, who had already commenced the work, and whose loss it was sought to supply by the talents of Holbein, recommended by Borbonius? in which case the publisher, well aware of the personally satirical character of some of the designs, may have thought it a good idea to attribute the whole of them to the dead man. The Creation and the Last Judgment, which differ in style from the rest of the devices, may, then, have been the work of Reperdius.

detail that especially distinguished the works of the great Basilean artist. The trees especially, when compared to those of Holbein in the next subject, are certainly weak in treatment; while Holbein, whose artistic comprehension of the forms and qualities of natural objects would not, it would seem, have placed the stars *upon* the clouds, instead of in the open spaces between them; while remarks of somewhat analogous character may be applied to the device representing the Last Judgment, which, however, exhibits more of the usual style of the handling of the great master.

It has been conjectured, and not without good show of collateral evidence, that Melchior and Gaspar Treschel, the publishers, were at the same time the engravers of this remarkable series, with the exception of the subject marked with a monogram of HL, which has been attributed to Lützenberger, the engraver of the almost equally celebrated alphabet with the same subjects. In support of this hypothesis it is urged that their names as engravers, "Melchior et Gaspar Treschel excudebant, Lugduni, 1538," occur at the end of the "Historiarum Veterum Instrumenti, Icones," etc., the drawings of which were by Holbein; while the verses, as in the "Dance of Death," are said to be by Gilles Corrozet. In conclusion, it should be stated that it has not been sought in any way to improve the somewhat rude form of the French verses in the present translations. They have indeed a quaint force and simplicity, which harmonizes well with similar qualities in the devices themselves, and are better, with all their rudeness, than many of those which accompanied most of the editions of this popular subject which succeeded the issue of the Holbein editions, and of which a brief general account will be found at the end of this volume. Many subsequent Lyonese editions of the "Simulacres et Historiées Faces de la Mort" successively appeared; first in 1542 (the Latin edition), the next being those of 1545, 1547, 1549, and 1552, several new subjects being successively added. The three editions which succeeded the Latin one contain twelve more subjects, which appear to be engraved by the same hand; but some of them do not strictly belong to the series in its original form. The boys at play, for instance, though said to represent the fatal vices—Gluttony, etc.—have not precisely the same significance as the original devices. In 1562 another edition appeared, with five more additional subjects, making in all seventeen additional devices; among which, in the true spirit of those of the first series, are the Soldier, the Gamblers, the Fool, the Robber, the Blind Man, the Waggoner, and the Beggar. I have not given facsimiles of these, as my present illustrations are confined to facsimiles of the devices which appeared in the first edition; and I have not alluded to the other subjects contained in the volume, such as the Medicina Animæ, which are without illustrations, and serve merely as the completion, or rather padding, of the book, and do not come within the scope of my present purpose.

With these observations I may close my brief introduction, and proceed to give some account and explanation of each subject in succession, remarking *en passant* that the present series of facsimiles are produced by the unerring process of photo-lithography, and are therefore infinitely more accurate reproductions than even the best of the many clever copies by hand which have already appeared.

THE SERIES OF FACSIMILES

FROM

HOLBEIN'S

DANCE OF DEATH.

Formauit DOMINVS DEVS hominem de limo
terræ,ad imaginē fuam creauit illum,mafculum & fœmis
nam creauit eos.

GENESIS I. & II.

DIEV, Ciel,Mer,Terre,procrea
De rien demonftrant fa puiffance
Et puis de la terre crea
L'homme,& la femme a fa femblance.

And the Lord God formed man of the dust of the ground.—*Genesis* ii. 7.

In the image of God created He him ; male and female created He them.—*Genesis* i. 27.

THE CREATION.

HETHER by Hans Holbein or some other hand, it must be admitted that in the restricted space of the present design the artist has contrived to introduce an epitome of the entire creation with great cleverness. The sun, the moon, the stars, the winds—each find their place. The "beasts of the field" are well represented by the ox, the stag, the ass, the bear, the rabbit in his burrow ; each full of distinctive character. The fowls of the air and the fish of the waters are not absent ; and even the lesser creatures,—the snail and the little lizard,—are not forgotten ; while the main feature of the composition—the creation of Eve during the deep sleep of Adam—is well conceived, and the intense repose of the sleeper wonderfully well expressed. This subject especially, and possibly the three which follow it, do not bear the impress of the Holbein pencil so strongly as the subsequent devices.

God made the Heavens, the Sea, the Earth.
O'er Chaos endless power displayed,
And from the dust—the dust of Earth—
Both man and woman in His Image made.

35

Quia audisti vocem vxoris tuæ,& comedisti
de ligno ex quo preceperam tibi ne come∫
deres &c.

GENESIS III

ADAM fut par EVE deceu
Et contre DIEV mangea la pomme,
Dont tous deux ont la Mort receu,
Et depuis fut mortel tout homme.

C

Because thou hast hearkened unto the voice of thy wife, and hast eaten of the tree, of which I commanded thee, saying, Thou shalt not eat of it.—*Genesis* iii. 17.

THE TEMPTATION.

HE superior artistic powers of this subject will be at once perceived on comparison with the first. The correct drawing of the figure of Adam, in the act of reaching an apple from the tree, is remarkable ; and the posture and general expression of Eve, who appears to be showing to Adam the apples, of which she has already tasted, and recommending their flavour, is very characteristic : even the mark where a piece has been bitten away from the one which she holds in her hand, is expressed with great care. Nevertheless, the unmistakeable impress of the Holbein genius does not force itself upon the critic, as in the succeeding subject.

The principal figures are closely surrounded by animals, which have, as yet, no fear of man.

When Adam was by Eve deceived,
And ate the fruit which God forbade,
They both the Doom of Death received,
And all man's race was mortal made.

Emisit eum DOMINVS DEVS de Para
diso voluptatis, vt operaretur terram de qua
sumptus est.

GENESIS IIT

DIEV chassa l'homme de plaisir
Pour uiure au labeur de ses mains:
Alors la Mort le uint saisir,
Et consequemment tous humains.

Therefore the Lord God sent him forth from
the garden of Eden, to till the ground from
whence he was taken.—*Genesis* iii. 23.

THE EXPULSION.

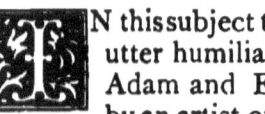N this subject the expression of abject terror and
utter humiliation delineated in the figures of
Adam and Eve, have rarely been surpassed
by an artist of the period; and the first appearance of Death upon the scene which he is to quit
no more, is strikingly managed. He is not about to
seize his prey at once, but comes furtively forth, in the
background, to observe with grinning satisfaction the
misery of his future prey, who are destined to become
the parents of a wide-spreading race of victims, while
he strikes the first chord of the lay by which he
will eventually summon them. The angel, energeti-
cally holding back the scabbard from which the
flaming sword has been suddenly drawn, is very grandly
conceived; but the details of the skeleton, especially
the expression of the head, scarcely reach, in energetic execution, those found in the regular series of
subjects.

So God drove man from Paradise,
By daily toil to win his bread ;
And Death came forth to claim his prize,
And number all men with the dead.

Maledicta terra in opere tuo, in laboribus comca
des cunctis diebus vitæ tuæ, donec reuerta
ris &c.

GENESIS III

Mauldicte en ton labeur la terre.
En labeur ta uie uferas,
Iufques que la Mort te foubterre.
Toy pouldre en pouldre tourneras.

C ij

Cursed is the ground for thy sake; in sorrow shalt thou eat of it all the days of thy life . . . . . and unto dust shalt thou return.—*Genesis* iii. 17 and 19.

THE CURSE OF DEATH.

THIS subject is sometimes called " Birth and Death," as representing the first mother with her first-born child, and the first days of human toil under the doom of Death. Eve, as sharer in the labours to which her race is condemned, holds the distaff even while she suckles her child, and Adam, with the first rude implements of husbandry—a mere branch, of suitable form—is endeavouring to uproot a tree of the primeval forest to make a space which he may till and sow with grain. An hour-glass stands behind him, indicating that for evermore his days are numbered ; while a grim skeleton working with him, denotes that thenceforth fallen man toils with Death at his elbow.

It should be borne in mind that this and the three preceding subjects, though not bearing the Holbein stamp so unmistakeably as the plates which follow, are yet very generally attributed to him.

Cursed in thy toil shall earth be found,
In labour shall thy days be pass'd ;
Till Death shall thrust thee underground,
Returning dust to dust at last.

Væ væ væ habitantibus in terra.

APOCALYPSIS VIII

Cuncta in quibus ſpiraculum vitæ eſt, mortua ſunt.

GENESIS VII

Malheureux qui uiuez au monde
Touſiours remplis d'aduerſitez,
Pour quelque bien qui uous abonde,
Serez tous de Mort uiſitez.

Woe! woe! woe! to the inhabiters of the earth.—*Revelation* viii. 13.

All in whose nostrils was the breath of life * * * * died.—*Genesis* vii. 22.

DEATH GOES FORTH.

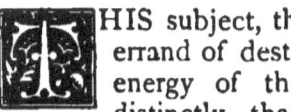HIS subject, the going forth of Death on his errand of destruction, exhibits the peculiar energy of the pencil of Holbein more distinctly than any similar features in the four preceding cuts, and the variety of instruments upon which the various skeletons are celebrating the preparation for the Dance has suggested the title of Death's Orchestra, by which the device is generally known, and which suggested to M. Kestner his work on the musical instruments represented in the various Dances of Death. Though among the most repulsive, this is at the same time one of the most grimly grand of the whole series of designs. Death, secure of his prey, holds his court in rampant triumph: the energy of the trombone-player, the smirking satisfaction of the performer on the hurdy-gurdy, and the frantic glee of the beater of the kettle-drum, are grimly grand, and horribly fantastic.

Woe! woe! inhabitants of Earth,
Where blighting cares so keenly strike,
And, spite of rank, or wealth, or worth,
Death—death will visit all alike.

Moriatur sacerdos magnus.
    IOSVE   XX
Et episcopatum eius accipiat alter.
  PSALMISTA   CVIII

Qui te cuydes immortel estre
Par Mort seras tost depesché,
Et combien que tu soys grand prebstre,
Vng aultre aura ton Euesché.

C iii

The death of the high priest that shall be in those days.—*Joshua* xx. 6.
Let another take his office.—*Psalm* cix. 8.

THE POPE.

THIS was invariably the first subject treated in the early editions of the "Danse Macabre." In the present device,—a great artistic advance upon its predecessors,—the Pope is summoned to his doom, by a lurking skeleton, at the very moment of his greatest exercise of sovereignty—while in the act of crowning a kneeling Emperor, who reverently kisses his foot. In this figure the artist has exhibited the pious humility of his favourite hero, the Emperor Maximilian, in contrast with the arrogant assumption of the Pope. A newly-created Cardinal stands at one side, and the designer, allowing his pencil to be influenced by the spirit of the Reformation, has represented the Bull issued on his nomination as being held over his head by a demon, while a mocking skeleton stands behind him, wearing a Cardinal's hat ; and another imp supports the draperies of the Papal throne.

Pride dreams an earthly immortality,
But death is certain—sudden to destroy ;
And even thou, high-priest, shalt surely die,
And a successor thy proud throne enjoy.

Difpone domui tuæ,morieris enim tu,& non viues.
ISAIÆ   XXXVIII
Ibi morieris,& ibi erit currus gloriæ tuæ.
ISAIÆ   XXII.

De ta maifon difpoferas
Comme de ton bien tranfitoire,
Car là ou mort repoferas,
Seront les chariotz de ta gloire.

Set thine house in order : for thou shalt die,
and not live."—*Isaiah* xxxviii. I.

There shalt thou die, and there the chariots
of thy glory shall be.—*Isaiah* xxii. 18.

THE EMPEROR.

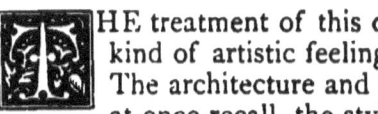 HE treatment of this composition is full of a
kind of artistic feeling peculiar to Holbein.
The architecture and canopies of the throne
at once recall the style of his work, as also
does the form of the " Antic Death," as Shakespeare
expresses it, who with grim alacrity is in the act of
discrowning the Emperor. The sovereign is here
represented in the act of calmly administering justice—though the term of his tenure of high office
having arrived is expressed by the broken blade of
the sword of justice, which he holds in his right hand.
It is evidently the Emperor Maximilian who is here
represented. The hour-glass placed close to the
orb and sceptre at his feet further indicates, also, that
the hour of quitting those symbols of power is at hand.

Order thine house while thou hast breath,
Bestow thy goods ; for thou must die,
And soon within the realms of Death
The chariots of thy state shall lie.

47

Sicut & rex hodie eſt,& cras morietur,nemo enim ex regibus aliud
habuit.

ECCLESIASTICI   X

Ainſi qu'auiourdhuy il eſt Roy,
Demain ſera en tombe cloſe.
Car Roy aulcun de ſon arroy
N'a ſceu emporter aultre choſe.

And he that is to-day a king, to-morrow shall die, &c. &c.—*Ecclesiasticus* x. 10.

THE KING.

N this composition the King is evidently Francis I. of France, who is intended to form a striking contrast to the Emperor Maximilian. His throne, sémé of fleurs-de-lis, the jaunty cap, or rather beret, and his well-known features, all serve to render the identity unmistakeable. His habitual dissipation is represented by the table, covered with the delicacies of a rich banquet, among which the artist has slipped the hour-glass, while Death himself pours out for him a copious libation of wine. It was this device, and its contrast with that of the Emperor, combined with a similar contrast exhibited between those representing the Queen and the Empress, which probably made it desirable to conceal the artist's name.

He who to-day is yet a king,
To-morrow shall entombèd be,
Nor carry with him anything
Of all his transient royalty.

Væ qui iuſtificatis impium pro mu
neribus,& iuſtitiam iuſti aufertu
ab eo.

E S A I E   V

Mal pour uous qui iuſtifiez
L'inhumain,& plain de maliçe,
Et par dons le ſanctifiez,
Oſtant au iuſte ſa iuſtice.

Woe unto them which justify the wicked for reward, and take away the righteousness of the righteous from him.—*Isaiah* v. 23.

THE CARDINAL.

HIS is, in every respect, a remarkable device. It has been observed that the text was evidently selected for the purpose of anathematizing the sale of "Indulgences;" and the Cardinal is possibly intended for Cajetan, in the act of selling a letter of Indulgence to a personage who extends his hand to receive it. On the other hand, it is possible that the document, with its many seals, represents the papal Bull by which the Cardinal represented in the device has been newly created, while Death strikes him in the very moment of his elevation. The publication of this series occurred just after Luther had been denounced by the Faculty of Theology of Paris, so that it is easy to conceive that an artist who had recently painted the portrait of Luther and his wife, should not wish his name to appear to a work in which the king of France and the dignitaries of the Church were so keenly satirized.

Woe unto ye, unjust, who justify
The wicked man, and shameful profit make,
Pretending his bad deeds to sanctify,
While from the just ye do all justice take.

Gradientes in superbia
poteſt Deus humilia-
re.

D A N I E.   I I I I

Qui marchez en pompe ſuperbe
La Mort vng iour uous pliera.
Cõme ſoubz uoz piedz ployez l'herbe,
Ainſi uous humiliera.

D

And those that walk in pride he is able to abase.—*Daniel* iv. 37.

THE EMPRESS.

IN this subject we have the Empress wearing the imperial crown. Death, in the garb' of an old and favoured courtier, leads her to the brink of an open grave, and taking her gently by the arm points down to it, as the end of all earthly grandeur. She receives the intimation with dignified composure ; and the staid propriety of her life is shown by the modestly coifed maidens, who accompany her in her walk, with the sedate demeanour of ladies who lead such lives as afford examples to their inferiors in rank.

This picture is evidently intended as a contrast and rebuke to the manners of the French court, as exhibited in the next subject. Maximilian, it is known, entertained the greatest hatred and resentment against France ; and as he was a great patron of artists, Holbein had probably known him as an early patron, and had imbibed many of his national antipathies.

Ye who walk forth in pomp superb,
Within brief space to Death must bow ;
As bends beneath the tread the herb,
Ye also must be trodden low.

Mulieres opulentæ surgite,& audite vocem
meam.Post dies,& annum,& vos contur-
· bemini.
ISAIÆ   XXXII

Leuez uous dames opulentes.
Ouyez la uoix des trespassez.
Apres maintz ans & iours passez,
Serez troublees & douloureses.

Rise up, ye women that are at ease: hear my voice. . . . . Many days and years shall ye be troubled.—*Isaiah* xxxii. 9, 10.

THE QUEEN.

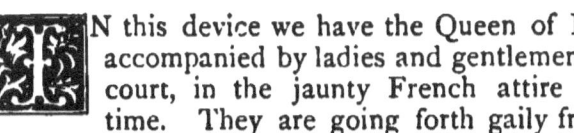N this device we have the Queen of France, accompanied by ladies and gentlemen of her court, in the jaunty French attire of the time. They are going forth gaily from the portico of a royal palace, when they are suddenly met by Death; not gravely, as in the case of the Empress, but full of capering antics; not in the dress of a wise counsellor, but in that of a court fool. He gleefully holds up the fatal hour-glass as he grasps the hand of his victim, the Queen; while the courtier, with true French politeness, attempts to defend the lady, holding her back by the arm, and endeavouring· to push aside the grizzly skeleton; but Death has taken his grasp too firmly to be shaken off; and the Queen, instead of patiently meeting her fate, is calling frantically for the help that cannot come. No wonder that the artist did not sign his name to devices of this kind, especially when published in France.

Daughters of rank and wealth, arise!
List to a warning from the dead;
After vain days and years mis-spent,
Come pangs that ye should learn to dread.

Percutiam paſtorem, & diſpergentur
oues.

XXVI   MAR.   XIIII

Le paſteur auſſi frapperay
Mitres & croſſes renuerſées.
Et lors quand ie l'attrapperay,
Seront ſes brebis diſperſées.

D ă

I will smite the shepherd, and the sheep shall be scattered.—*St. Mark* xiv. 27.

THE BISHOP.

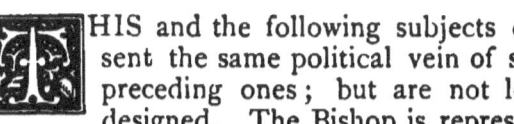

HIS and the following subjects do not present the same political vein of satire as the preceding ones; but are not less cleverly designed. The Bishop is represented walking forth in a beautiful summer evening, among his flock—as expressed by a flock of actual sheep, most carefully and correctly drawn. The sun is setting gorgeously behind a mountain; but the Bishop is not aware that it foreshadows the close of his life as well as the close of the day, until Death sets down the hour-glass in front of him, with all the sand run out, and leads him gently away.

The pastor from his sheep I'll take;
Mitre and crosier cast to ground;
And when the shepherd I o'ertake,
The scatter'd flock shall scarce be found.

57

Princeps induetur mœrore.Et
quiefcere faciam fuperbiã po
tentium.

EZECHIE.   VII

Vien,prince,auec moy,& delaiffe
Honneurs mondains toft finiffantz.
Seule fuis qui,certes,abaiffe
L'orgueil & pompe des puiffantz.

The Prince shall be clothed with desolation. I will also make the pomp of the strong to cease.—*Ezekiel* vii. 24 and 27.

THE PRINCE ELECTOR.

EATH lays his resistless hand upon the ermined cape of the Prince, whose fate is thus sealed, while a poor beggar woman, not dreaming that princes are subject to the common lot, still continues to supplicate alms. The robes of the Prince are designed in the simple manner peculiar to Holbein, who never adopted the florid treatment of drapery by means of those richly-varied crinkles and angular foldings which Albert Durer, Lucas Cranach, and other contemporary artists of the German school adopted. It will be observed that the hour-glass, with its sands run out, fills a niche in the palace tower, instead of a statue.

Come, potent prince, with me alone—
Leave transient pomps of worldly state ;
I am the one who can fling down
The pride and honours of the great.

·Ipſe morietur. Qyda nõ habuit diſci⸗
plinam,& in multitudine ſtultitiæ
ſuæ decipietur.
P R O V E R. . V

Il mourra,Car il n'a receu
En ſoy aulcune diſcipline,
Et au nombre ſera deceu
De folie qui le domine.

D iij

He shall die without instruction, and in the greatness of his folly he shall go astray.

Proverbs v. 23.

THE MITRED ABBOT.

THIS is one of those grand burlesques which Paul Lacroix would characterize as "sublime buffoonery." It represents the Mitred Abbot, long revelling in lazy luxury, suddenly summoned by the grim skeleton. His obese form and heavy cheeks and chin mark him out at once as a bad type of his class, and are most expressively drawn. In his terror he holds up a richly-bound Book of Hours by way of defence or as a sign of authority, and attempts to push the unwelcome intruder aside ; but Death dances carelessly off with his victim, in very wantonness of triumph donning the mitre and crosier of the doomed abbot ; the whole attitude of the skeleton being a marvellous display of the artist's powers in treating such combinations of the horrible and the burlesque. The exhausted hour-glass, as usual, tells its ominous tale, being slyly placed by the artist on the branch of a tree, immediately over the head of the victim.

He dies, and he has never learned
The discipline that points the way
To the true life—while he has turned
To lusts that lead the soul astray.

·Laudaui magis mortuos quàm
viuentes.

ECCLE.　IIII

l'ay touſiours les mortz plus loué
Que les uifz,eſquelz mal abonde,
Toutesfoys la Mort ma noué
Au ranc de ceulx qui ſont au monde.

Wherefore I praised the dead which are already dead more than the living which are yet alive.—*Ecclesiastes* iv. 2.

THE LADY ABBESS.

HIS clever and characteristic device is described by some as, simply, the Nun ; but, following, as it does, that of the Abbot, I am inclined to regard it as referring to a Lady Abbess, especially on account of the crosier, which still rests between her arms, though she has let go her hold upon it in the action of clasping her hands in supplication, while still holding her rosary. In the appended verses she is made to plead that she has been very civil to Death in praising the dead more than the living ; but the weak appeal is fruitless, and he drags her off by a convenient portion of her monastic habiliment. The convent doorway with its swinging bell, the screaming sister, and the similarly appropriate accessories of the other devices, tend to make this series the most remarkable among the many analogous productions of the artists of the fifteenth and sixteenth centuries.

The dead, she urged, I'm ever praising
More than the living, who in sin are found ;
And yet, in Death's o'er-rude appraising,
I'm rank'd with worldly sinners who abound.

Quis eſt homo qui viuet,& non videbit
mortem,eruet animã ſuam de manu
inferi?

P S A L.   L X X X V I I I

Qui eſt celluy, tant ſoit grand homme,
Qui puiſſe uiure ſans mourir?
Et de la Mort,qui tout aſſomme,
Peut ſon âme à ſoy recourir?

What man is he that liveth, and shall not
see Death? Shall he deliver his soul from the
hand of the grave?—*Psalm* lxxxix. 48.

THE NOBLEMAN.

E have here a very striking composition : a
Noble Knight stalwart in build, and brim-
ful of defiance to every kind of danger, has
had his footsteps dogged by Death, who,
meaning work, has brought an ambulance or bier along
with him, upon which stands the significant hour-glass.
The powerfully-limbed knight seizes his enemy by the
throat, and swings his great sword above his head for
such a blow as might crash through and shiver the
helmet of a human opponent like an egg-shell ; yet,
something in the position of the arm tells that its
power is paralyzed, and that the threatened blow can
never descend ; while Death, tightening his grasp,
leaves us in no doubt as to his victory. It is as the
small spider seizing on the giant fly, who buzzes and
struggles and beats his wings in vain, till he is webbed
into the toils of his destroyer.

Who is the man, however strong or great,
Who can escape the final destiny ?—
Who can avoid the dark and awful gate,
Or cheat grim Death of certain victory ?

Ecce appropinquat ho-
ra.

MAT. XXVI

Tu uas au choeur dire tes heures
Priant Dieu pour toy, & ton proche,
Mais il fault ores que tu meures.
Voy tu pas l'heure qui approche?

Behold, the hour is at hand.—*St. Matthew*
xxvi. 45.

THE CANON.

IN this device the rich Canon, attended by
his falconer, is summoned to his fate as he is
entering the church to perform his usual devotions. The grim smile with which Death
holds the hour-glass in front of him, as he walks
towards the portal, is very strikingly managed, and
the prominent aspect of the ominous symbol thus
held in front of him, defining itself with impressive
distinctness against a broad light on one of the stone
columns, is very artistically devised.

The easy and luxurious lives of the Canons, who
held a sort of semi-ecclesiastical position, is well illustrated in George Sands' striking story of Consuelo.

In choir each day thou mutterest prayer;
To-day that muttering may not be;
Thou must e'en die—all unaware,
Behold! 'tis time; so come with me!

Disperdam iudicem de medio
eius.

A M·O S   I I

Du mylieu d'eulx uous osteray
Iuges corrumpus par presentz. ·
Point ne serez de Mort exemptz.
Car ailleurs uous transporteray.

F:

And I will cut off the Judge from the midst thereof.—*Amos* ii. 3.

THE UNJUST JUDGE.

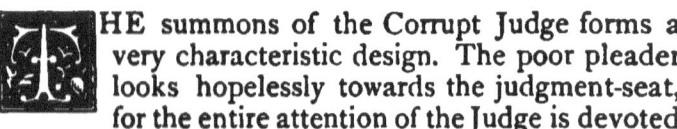THE summons of the Corrupt Judge forms a very characteristic design. The poor pleader looks hopelessly towards the judgment-seat, for the entire attention of the Judge is devoted to the appellant of superior wealth, who is in the act of taking money from his wallet, to place in the extended palm of the Judge, when Death, flinging down his hour-glass in sheer disgust, leaps behind the Judge's seat, and is seen in the act of wrenching from him that staff of office which he is destined to require no more.

From out thy seat thou shalt be taken,
So oft bribed to iniquity—
Thy ill-got gains must be forsaken;
No bribe can buy thy life of me.

Callidus vidit malum,& abſcōdit ſe
innocens,pertranſi;t,& afflictus eſt
damno.
PROVER. XXII

L'homme cault a ueu la malice
Pour l'innocent faire obliger,
Et puis par uoye de iuſtice
Liſt uenu le pauure affliger.

A prudent man foreseeth the evil, and hideth himself; but the simple pass on, and are punished.—*Proverbs* xxii. 3.

THE ADVOCATE.

THE verses of the French author are extremely obscure, and appear almost like a misunderstood translation of the Latin text, to which the English translation has been made to adhere somewhat more closely. The subject evidently represents an Advocate in the act of receiving a fee from a rich client; but in the moment of satisfaction at being well paid for pleading the cause of the rich against the poor, Death suddenly holds above his head the fatal hour-glass, while a poor beggar clasps his hands in despair, at the sight of so much gold at a time when he is both cold and hungry, and would gladly change places with the Advocate, little dreaming that in another moment the man whose position he envies would be but too glad to change places with him; for life is still dearer than gold.

The cautious man, with malice ever keen,
The simpler in his grasp will tightly bind
By legal cunning, and has ever been
The hard oppressor of his poorer kind.

Qui obturat aurem fuam ad clamorem
pauperis,& ipfe clamabit,& non exau=
dietur.

P R O V E R.   X X·I

Les riches confeillez toufiours,
Et aux pauures clouez l'oreille.
Vous crierez aux derniers iours,
Mais Dieu uous fera la pareille.

E ij

Whoso stoppeth his ears at the cry of the poor, he also shall cry himself, but shall not be heard.—*Proverbs* xxi. 13.

THE COUNSELLOR.

THE poet and designer, while aiming their shafts of satire at all classes in this striking series of subjects, have been more hard upon the churchman and the lawyer than any other classes. Here is another hit at the legal profession, somewhat analogous to that of the last device, but more severe. The legal Counsellor is in such deep consultation with a rich merchant, that he does not in the least perceive the pleading of the poor beggar, who is plucking at his richly furred cloak. A demon-imp is at the same moment blowing astute advice into his ear, which he communicates to his rich client. In the mean time Death has crept in between the lawyer and the dealer, and, all unseen, holds up the hour-glass in token that the time is at hand, and is also furnished with a sexton's spade, denoting that the summons is immediate, and a grave required without delay.

Ye rich, who cautious counsel take on gain,
Ye cannot hear the starving poor man sue ;
But, at the last, ye too will cry in vain,
And God will turn as deaf an ear to you.

Væ qui dicitis malum bonum,& bonum malū,
ponentes tenebras lucem,& lucem tenebras,
ponentes amarum dulce,& dulce in amarum.

ISAIÆ. XV

Mal pour uous qui ainſi oſez
Le mal pour le bien nous blaſmer,
Et le bien pour mal expoſez,
Mettant auec le doulx l'amer. .

Woe unto them that call evil good, and good evil ; that put darkness for light, and light for darkness ; that put bitter for sweet, and sweet for bitter.—*Isaiah* v. 20.

THE PREACHER.

HIS satirical criticism of the Preacher represents the antagonistic feelings of a period of transition. With the Reformer, the preacher, putting "darkness before light," would represent the Romish priest, while a Papist would at once interpret the device in his fashion, as representing the innovative Reformer. In either case Death is in attendance, claiming his victim in the midst of his ministrations. The device has evidently been conceived in a Protestant spirit, for the skeleton wears, in mockery, the stole of the Roman Catholic priest ; and exhibits above the head of the doomed preacher the closed jaws of a skull, which will never more open to emit the sound of a human voice. The artistic treatment of the congregation, from the man dropping off to sleep against the pulpit, to the smallest of the figures in the more distant groups, is most masterly and characteristic in design.

Woe unto ye who do profanely dare
Evil for good to show, by praise or blame ;
And, also, good things evil ones declare,
And sweet for bitter falsely do proclaim.

Sum quidem & ego mortalis
homo.

SAP. VII

Ie porte le ſainct ſacrement
Cuidant le mourant ſecourir,
Qui mortel ſuis pareiſlement.
Et comme luy me fault mourir.

E iň

Myself also am a mortal man.—*Wisdom of Solomon*, vii. 1.

THE LAST SACRAMENT.

THIS subject is not one of the least ingeniously conceived, though perhaps less attractive and striking in artistic execution than many others. The action of the skeleton is, however, quite a masterpiece of grim humoristic design. A priest has been called out in the night to administer the last sacrament, and Death is roused to the briskest state of gleeful alacrity. The handiness with which he carries the church lantern in one hand, and with the other rings the bell, announcing the approach of the sacrament, while he deftly tucks his hour-glass under his arm, is matchless in sardonic humour. The Priest, and the attendant acolyte with the holy water, exhibit the undisturbed equanimity of practised officials, in strong contrast with the bowed head and grief-stricken face of the young woman, perhaps the wife or daughter of the dying man, who has been to fetch the Priest.

The holy sacrament I bear with me
To soothe the sinner in his latest hour,
I, who am mortal too, as well as he,
And can no more than he evade Death's
    power.

Sedentes in tenebris , & in vm=
bra mortis, vinctos in mendi=
citate.

P S A L.   C·V I

Toy qui n'as foucy, ny remord
Sinon de ta mendicité,
Tu fierras a l'umbre de Mort
Pour t'ouster de necessité.

Such as sit in darkness and in the shadow of death, being bound in affliction.—*Psalm* cvii. 10.

THE MENDICANT FRIAR.

THE begging Brother is returning to his convent after a successful round among the pious supporters of monastic principles, as his well-filled wallet sufficiently indicates; when, just as he reaches the entrance, he is ruthlessly seized by Death, from whose grasp he struggles vigorously to free himself, at the same time clinging tightly to the begging money-box, which he holds out at arm's length from his pursuer, as far as he can reach. But the energy of Death in the struggle is of so determined a character that there is evidently no chance for the doomed brother, who is roaring loudly, but in vain, for mercy.

The passage selected as a motto from the Psalms, in the version of the Vulgate, "vinctos in mendicitate," is more appropriate than the English translation, which renders the passage "being bound in affliction."

Thou who hast never felt remorse nor care,
Beyond the craft of thy mendicity,
Within the shades of death I now will bear,
To save thee from such base necessity.

Est via quæ videtur homini iusta: nouissi-
ma autem eius deducunt hominem ad
mortem.
PROVER. IIII

Telle uoye aux humains est bonne,
Et a l'homme tresiuste semble.
Mais la fin d'elle a l'homme donne,
La Mort, qui tous pecheurs assemble,

There is a way which seemeth right unto a man, but the ends thereof are the ways of death.—*Proverbs* xiv. 12.

THE CANONESS.

THE Canoness is sometimes incorrectly described as the Nun. There were certain canonries to which ladies of rank, professing a life celibacy, but without taking the vows, were eligible, and many scandals were circulated concerning them. The most recent example of a scandalous appointment was perhaps that of Lolah Montez, appointed by King Louis I. to a rich canonry in Bavaria. In this composition the Canoness is diverted from her devotions by a youth who sits near, singing to the accompaniment of a kind of lute; while at the very moment Death, with his bony fingers, extinguishes the lights on the altar; thus symbolizing the extinction of the human life, which he is also come to effect. May not Shakespeare have had this device in his mind when penning the passage in which Othello, determining to kill Desdemona, exclaims, " Put out the light—and then—put out the light."

Ill ways to human ken seem right,
Frail pleasures neither bad nor vain ;
But Death they bring, with fatal blight,
Who yokes all sinners in his train.

Melior eſt mors quàm
vita.

ECCLE.   XXX

En peine ay ueſcu longuement
Tant que nay plus de uiure enuie,
Mais bien ie croy certainement,
Meilleure la Mort que la uie.

Death is better than a bitter life.—*Ecclesiasticus* xxx. 17.

THE AGED WOMAN.

THE treatment of this subject has evidently been carefully considered. There is no violent seizing of the prey, as in the case of the robust mendicant friar, and others. On the contrary, Death comes as her friend; he takes her gently by the arm to afford that support which her tottering steps require, and for which her own tremblingly-held walking-stick scarcely suffices : and he wears a funeral wreath to cover the ghastliness of his bare skull. Indeed he appears to occupy himself entirely with the comfortable transit of his aged victim, leaving to an assistant skeleton the task of the music, who is executing an evidently vivacious air on the dulcimer. We are shown, too, that it is no longer of any use even to measure the duration of such a decayed life, for the very hour-glass in the corner is represented as worn out and broken.

The love of life has ceased in thee,
Who long hast known this suffering strife ;
Then come along to rest with me,
For death is better now than life.

Medice, cura te
ipſum.

LVCÆ IIII

Tu congnoys bien la maladie
Pour le patient ſecourir,
Et ſi ne ſcais teſte eſtourdie,
Le mal dont tu deburas mourir.

F

Physician, heal thyself.—*Luke* iv. 23.

THE PHYSICIAN.

THIS is one of the most ingenious compositions of the whole series. Death steps in between the Doctor and his patient. " This poor creature is already mine," Death seems to say, as he gently clasps a hand nearly as attenuated and bony as his own ; while with his other hand he mockingly presents to the Doctor a large phial, the contents of which the learned man carefully scrutinizes. He has never yet examined such a compound as that which is now presented to him, and of which he evidently mistrusts the nature. It may symbolize the last strong sedative from which none revive. The book-shelf and other accessories are very truthfully drawn and engraved, yet without any of that stiff and uncouth realism which is just now the prevailing fashion with a class of artists who are servilely imitating the forms, while misconceiving the spirit, of the early quattrocentisti and their followers.

Ailments thou understandest well,
And healer of the sick canst be ;
But rash, vain man, thou canst not tell
In what form Death shall come to thee.

85

Indica mihi fi nofti omnia. Sciebas qudd
nafciturus effes, & numerum dierum
tuorum noueras?
J O B   X X V I I I

Tu dis par Amphibologie
Ce qu'aux aultres doibt aduenir,
Dy moy donc par Aftrologie
Quand tu deburas a moy uenir?

Knowest thou it because thou wast then born, or because the number of thy days is great?—*Job* xxxviii. 21.

THE ASTROLOGER.

THIS design is interesting, no less for the characteristic conception and drawing of the two figures, Death and the Astrologer, than for the beautifully designed ornaments of the rich furniture of the room, which exhibits the rich decorative taste of the time in a very successful manner. The attitude of the Astrologer, seated, with a well-assumed air of gravity, in his official chair, and pointing to the suspended spheres as he is supposed to be setting forth the events of the future, is suddenly interrupted by Death, who, by the author of the appended verses, is made to exclaim, tauntingly, "Thou tellest to others by phrases of double meaning (amphibology), that which will happen to them ; tell me then by astrology, when thou art doomed to come to me." The mocking position of Death, holding out a skull towards his victim, as a symbol of death, instead of the usual hour-glass, is very striking.

Thou tell'st by amphibology
That which to others shall befall,
Then tell me by astrology
When *thou* shalt answer to my call.

Stulte hac nocte repetunt animam tuam, & quæ parasti cuius erunt?

LVCÆ   XII

Ceste nuict la Mort te prendra,
Et demain seras enchassé.
Mais dy moy, sol, a qui uiendra
Le bien que tu as amassé?

F ij

Thou fool, this night thy soul shall be required of thee.—*Luke* xii. 20.

THE MISER.

HERE is one of the most powerfully conceived subjects of the whole series. The thickness of the walls, and the ponderously double-barred window of the gold-lover's retreat, are represented as amply sufficient to keep out ordinary thieves; but one has glided in to whom bolts and bars are no impediment. The unceremonious visitor seats himself at the table covered with gold, and with a sudden feeling of grim drollery, helps himself to large handfuls of the abounding coin, to the horror and astonishment of the miser, who either sees, or instinctively feels, that his hoards are slipping away from him, and throws up his arms in direst dismay; perceiving that even the strongly-clamped and double-padlocked chests can no longer preserve to him a single ounce of his dearly loved gold, for he hears a mysterious voice whispering to him, "Who shall now inherit all the wealth thou hast amassed?"

This very night shalt thou know Death!
To-morrow be encoffined fast!
Then tell me, fool! while thou hast breath,
Who'll have the gold thou hast amassed?

Qui congregat thefauros mendacij vanus
& excors eft , & impingetur ad laqueos
mortis.

P.ROVER. XXI

Vain eft cil qui amaffera
Grandz biens,& trefors pour mentir,,
La Mort l'en fera repentir.
Car, en fes lacz furpris fera..

The getting of treasures by a lying tongue is a vanity tossed to and fro of them that seek death.—*Proverbs* xxi. 6.

THE MERCHANT.

THE usual features of the quay of a busy sea-port form the accessories and background of this composition, and exhibit wonderful variety and richness of detail, in so restricted a space. In the foreground are casks and bales pencilled with a precision and accuracy seldom surpassed in specimens of the best modern drawing. In the front is a great and heavy bale, which has been evidently moved to its present position on rollers, to serve as an impromptu table, on which the Merchant is in the act of paying or receiving money in settlement of accounts, when he is suddenly summoned to his own last account, to the consternation of the participator in the pending transactions, who rushes away in a well-conceived attitude of extreme alarm. The summons is supposed to be so sudden, that even the hour-glass has not been brought forward as a warning.

The Merchant's wealth's a worthless thing,
Of others, won by lies, the spoils ;
But Death will sure repentance bring,
Snaring the snarer in his toils.

Qui volunt diuites fieri incidunt in laqueum
diaboli,& defideria multa,& nociua, quæ
mergunt homines in interitum.

I   AD TIMO.   VI

Pour acquerir des biens mondains
Vous entrez en tentation,
Qui uous met es perilz foubdains,
Et uous maine a perdition.

F

But they that will be rich fall into temptation and a snare, and into many foolish and
hurtful lusts, which drown men in destruction
and perdition.—1 *Timothy* vi. 9.

THE SHIPWRECK.

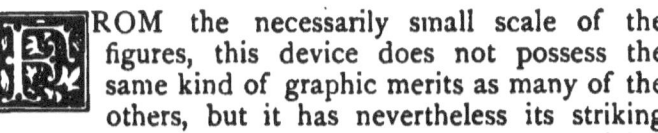ROM the necessarily small scale of the
figures, this device does not possess the
same kind of graphic merits as many of the
others, but it has nevertheless its striking
features. The sail torn to shreds by the driving
storm, and the appearance of rain and wind against
the sky, are well rendered. The action of Death, in
apparently endeavouring to prevent the fall of the
broken mast, is not very obvious, though it may be
intended to express that Death himself is shocked at
the wholesale harvest of victims so suddenly brought
within his grasp, and seeks to spare some of the
doomed ones thus cast by adventurous greed of gain
into his clutches. The desperation of those who prepare to leap into the raging sea to escape the lesser
dangers of the straining vessel, and of those within it
who throw up their arms, imploring help that can never
reach them, are vigorously though simply expressed.

To gain the good things of this world,
What risks are dared without contrition.
Seas braved! and treacherous sails unfurl'd!
So men rush on to their perdition.

Subito morientur, & in media nocte turbabuntur populi, & auferent violentum absq̃ manu.

IOB   XXXIIII

Peuples foubdain f'efleueront
A lencontre de l'inhumain,
Et le uiolent ofteront
D'auec eulx fans force de main.

In a moment shall they die, and the people shall be troubled at midnight, and pass away, and the mighty shall be taken away without hand.—*Job* xxxiv. 20.

THE KNIGHT.

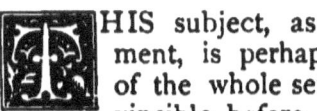HIS subject, as regards the artistic treatment, is perhaps one of the most powerful of the whole series. The Knight, while invincible before his adversaries in front, is suddenly slain by an unexpected thrust from behind. In vain he fiercely turns half round and seizes the lance by which he is being transfixed ; Death, *in propriâ personâ*, being the enemy who has made the thrust with such deadly force and accuracy, that it has passed clean through the steel-plate armour. The action of the grinning skeleton, with his cape of mail and cuirass,—his thigh-pieces swung back from the fleshless bones by his grotesque energy, is a piece of burlesque tragedy of a very terrible and striking kind. The hour-glass is made to play its symbolic part with great effect in this composition, as an emblem of sudden destruction—its sands have not run out, but it is cast down and rendered useless.

E'en in a moment shall they die,
At midnight shall men quake with fear,
The mighty shall not be pass'd by,
Nor know who thrusts the fatal spear.

Quoniam cùm interierit non fumet fe-
cum omnia, neq; cum eo defcëdet glo
ria eius.

PSAL.   XLVIII

Auec foy rien n'emportera,
Mais qu'une foys la Mort le tombe,
Rien de fa gloire n'oftera,
Pour mettre auec foy en fa tombe.

For when he dieth he shall take nothing away, his glory shall not descend after him.—*Psalm* xlix. 17.

THE COUNT.

THE finely designed figure representing the Count suddenly summoned to quit his earthly state, is attired in the splendid costume of the nobles of the court of Maximilian, so familiar to the curious through Burgmair's. famous prints of the triumphs of that prince. Death, while seizing the shield of the doomed count, the symbol of his nobility, makes his contempt more bitter by assuming the attire of a peasant, an ignoble despised peasant, who also treads recklessly on the heraldic trappings of a helmet which lies on the ground ; the victim being rudely told, in this humiliating fashion, that he may carry none of the symbols of his earthly state with him to the grave. A small fortified town is seen in the distance, with its château-fort and church, representing the chief seat of his pride and power, and which furnished, perhaps, his name and title, but to which he will return no more.

Baubles and earthly pomps for ever flown,
Poor as the poorest he hath swiftly grown,
Yet shall good deeds, if any he hath done,
Remain his glory after he is gone.

Spiritus meus attenuabitur, dies mei bre-
uiabuntur, & solum mihi superest sepul-
chrum.

IOB   XVII

Mes esperitz sont attendriz,
Et ma uie s'en ua tout beau.
Las mes longz iours sont amoindriz,
Plus ne me reste qu'un tombeau.

My breath is corrupt, my days are extinct, the graves are ready for me.—*Job* xvii. 1.

THE OLD MAN.

THE bent figure of the aged man, his head sunk almost below his shoulders, and that of Death, who guides him gently towards an open grave in a cemetery, while playing an air upon an instrument resembling a cithara, are both strikingly conceived. That of the old man must, indeed, have been floating in the artistic mind of Rethel when he composed his celebrated " Death the Friend" as a companion to his "Death the Enemy." There is a calmness in the general treatment of this subject, which forms a very soothing contrast to the grim energy and sardonic hilarity with which the destroyer subdues his more robust and obstinate victims.

My spirit weakens day by day,
My life has reached its latest stave,
My latter days pass fast away—
Nothing awaits me but the grave.

Ducunt in bonis dies fuos,&
in puncto ad inferna de=
fcendunt.

IOB   XXI

En biens mõdains leurs iours defpendẽt
En uoluptez,& en trifteffe,
Puis foubdain aux Enfers defcendent,
Ou leur ioye paffe en trifteffe.

G

They spend their days in wealth, and in a
moment go down to the grave.—*Job* xxi. 13.

THE COUNTESS.

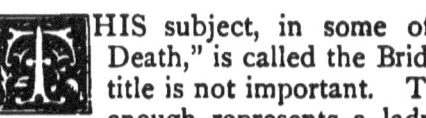HIS subject, in some of the "Dances of
Death," is called the Bride. But the special
title is not important. The design evidently
enough represents a lady belonging to the
higher social ranks, who is devoted to worldly
vanities, and more especially those of dress. A
tirewoman is in the act of bringing to her a richly-
garnished robe, in which she evidently contemplates
adorning herself, when Death, who has surrepti-
tiously introduced himself, to claim his victim, places
upon her neck, with truly demoniac playfulness, a
necklace formed of human bones, held together by
interlacing worms, just as though he were an obse-
quious jeweller seeking the patronage of the great lady
for a necklace, which he grinningly seems to describe
as of exquisitely suitable character to the occasion.
The hour-glass, placed among the toilet luxuries, plays
its part with even more than ordinary significance.

In worldly ways their days are spent,
In idle pleasures,—longings vain,
When, sudden, to their doom they're cast,
And their brief joys are changed to pain.

Me & te fola mors fepa-
rabit.

RVTH.   I

Amour qui unyz nous faict uiure,
En foy noz cueurs preparera,
Qui long temps ne nous pourra fuyure,
Car la Mort nous feparera.

If ought but death part thee and me.—*Ruth* i. 17.

THE BRIDE AND BRIDEGROOM.

HE treatment of this subject is rendered interesting by the careful manner in which the rich costume of the day is represented, as well as by the general composition, which, though simple, is very effective. In this instance it is not intended that Death should be absolutely seizing upon the bride or bridegroom as they return from the altar, as is the case in other series, in which the image of Death is represented in the act of tearing them asunder ; but, on the contrary, he is only present in the form of a warning, that, however great their happiness may be, it must end in eventual separation, though the time may yet be distant, as indicated by the hour-glass, in which the sands of life are still plentiful in the upper part.

The love by which they are united,
By faith should teach them, ere too late,
That soon such unions may be blighted,
And Death step in to separate.

De lectulo super quem ascendi=
sti non descendes , sed morte
morieris.

    ]]] [REG.   I

Du lict sus lequel as monté
Ne descendras a ton plaisir.
Car Mort t'aura tantost dompté,
Et en brief te uiendra saisir.

                        G ij

Thou shalt not come down from that bed on which thou art gone up, but shalt surely die.— 2 *Kings* i. 4.

THE DUCCHESS.

HIS subject is, perhaps, the least successfully treated of the whole of this series, and yet the design is in many respects so artistic that it can scarcely be considered the work of an inferior hand. The difficult position of the figure, in the act of preparing to lie down, is well managed, and the action of Death tugging at the bed-clothes is extremely graphic, the figure being rendered more ghastly by the long hair still adhering to the skull, indicating, possibly, that it is that of a once beautiful woman. The head of the skeleton playing the violin is rendered more grim and terrible in its aspect by being placed in the *shade*,—the form of the dark skull coming out strongly against a white wall. This engraving has the initials H. L., a mark which has led to much discussion, but which may possibly be that of the engraver, and not that of the artist ; the treatment of the cutting being in fact somewhat different.

Thou ne'er shalt leave that bed of down,
On which thou art about to lie.
Death round thee hath his meshes thrown,
And, vain one! thou must surely die.

Venite ad me qui onerati
eſtis.

MATTH.   XI

Venez,& apres moy marchez
Vous qui eſtes par trop charge.
C'eſt aſſez ſuiuy les marchez:
Vous ſerez par moy decharge.

Come unto me, all ye that labour and are heavy laden.—*Matthew* xi. 28.

THE PEDLAR.

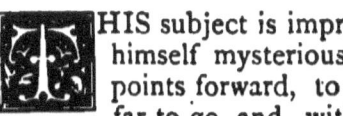HIS subject is impressively treated. Feeling himself mysteriously held back, the Pedlar points forward, to indicate that he has still far to go, and, with an appealing look, turns back his labour-lined face entreating that he may not be interrupted. But Death holds his sleeve with a grip that is not to be shaken off, while a second skeleton is playing on a rude stringed instrument, the parting knell of the victim. The aspect of the road across a dreary country, only varied by a simple roadside altar, with a small niche for the figure of a saint, is very characteristic, as is also the heavy pack, piled up with rolls of linen and other wares, of the weight of which Death is about to relieve the overloaded wayfarer for ever. It should be observed, that with the poor, Death is nearly always represented as bringing relief.

Cease from thy tramping—follow me ;
Thou'rt heavy laden for the road.
Ay ! let the fair and market be ;
I will thy weighty pack unload.

In ſudore vultus tui veſceris pane
tuo.

GENS.   I

A la ſueur de ton uiſaige
Tu gaigneras ta pauure uie.
Apres long trauail,& uſaige,
Voicy la Mort qui te conuie.

G iij

In the sweat of thy face shalt thou eat bread till thou return unto the ground.—*Genesis* iii. 19.

THE PLOUGHMAN.

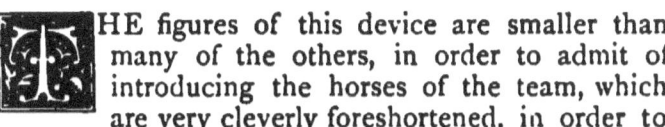

HE figures of this device are smaller than many of the others, in order to admit of introducing the horses of the team, which are very cleverly foreshortened, in order to bring them well into the picture. Death is acting as teamster, flourishing his whip, and dancing along at his work, as though with a thorough enjoyment of the feeling that the old Ploughman was doing his last day's work. The heavy step of the worn-out tiller of the soil, and the seeming effort with which he guides and steadies the plough, are inimitably expressed. The sun, setting behind the tower of the village church, emblematic of a closing life, as well as of a closing day, plays the part usually assigned to the hour-glass.

With sweating brow and horny hand,
Thou work'st ere thou mayst break thy fast:
Enough thou'st till'd and delved the land;
Death comes to speed thy plough at last.

Homo natus de muliere, breui viuens tempore
repletur multis miserijs, qui quasi flos egre‑
ditur, & conteritur, & fugit velut ymbra.

      I O B   X I I I I

Tout homme de la femme yssant
Remply de misere, & d'encombre,
Ainsi que fleur tost finissant.
Sort & puis fuyt comme faict l'umbre.

Man that is born of a woman is of few days,
and full of trouble. He cometh forth like a
flower, and is cut down ; he fleeth also as a
shadow, and continueth not.—*Job* xiv. i.

THE YOUNG CHILD.

HIS subject forms a remarkable termination
to the series. Death has been exhibited
striking down his victims in youth, in man-
hood, and in old age ; and at last even the
little child at play before the cheerful fire, is being
dragged forth from the poor cottage by the grim
visitant, before the eyes of the terror-stricken mother,
even while she is in the very act of preparing for
her youngest darling a meal, of which he is never to
taste. Nothing can be more dramatic than the treatment of this scene ; Death wears the loose cap of a
peasant, and affects to lead forth the infant affection-
ately, as though he were its father ; while an elder
child, to whose eyes, perhaps, the skeleton is invisible,
screams with terror at the mysterious disappearance
of his little brother.

All men that are of woman born,
Are of few days, of toil and pain ;
They are like flowers with grass down shorn ;
Like shadows—never seen again.

Omnes ftabimus ante tribunal domini.
ROMA.   XIIII
Vigilate,& orate,quia nefcitis qua hora
venturus fit dominus.
MAT.   XXIIII

Deuant le trofne du grand iuge
Chafcun de foy compte rendra,
Pourtant ueillez,qu'il ne uous iuge.
Car ne fcauez quand il uiendra.

For we shall all stand before the judgment seat of Christ.—*Romans* xiv. 10.

Watch therefore ; for ye know not what hour your Lord doth come.—*Matthew* xxiv. 42.

THE LAST JUDGMENT.

IT has been thought by some critics that this device, and that of the Creation, are not the work of the same hand as those of most others of this series. But this may possibly be a somewhat hasty conclusion, for the nature of the subjects evidently necessitated a different treatment, the cause of which need not necessarily be sought in the supposition that they are the work of another hand, which. however, may possibly be the case. It may be remarked that the heavenly sphere, spanned by the well-known emblem of the "bow that was set in the clouds," and having the lesser sphere of the earth seen within it, is one of the favourite methods of the artists of the 15th and 16th centuries, for representing heaven and earth in their symbolical designs.

Before the judgment seat of power
Shall each with his account appear.
Watch, then!—for thou know'st not the hour
In which thou mayst be summoned there.

Memorare nouiſſima,&
in æternum non pec-
cabis.

    ECCLE.   VII

Si tu ueulx uiure ſans peché
Voy ceſte imaige a tous propos,
Et point ne ſeras empeſché,
Quand tu t'en iras a repos.

Whatsoever thou takest in hand, remember the end, and thou shalt never do wrong.— *Ecclesiasticus* vii. 36.

THE MEMENTO MORI.

THIS ingeniously devised tail-piece is as full of pointed symbolism as any subject in the series. The broken shield with the death's-head for its sole blazon, is a powerfully conceived emblem of the transitory character of earthly rank and state,—an idea still farther carried out by the crest above the helmet, which consists of an hour-glass as an emblem of life ; above which, two skeleton arms raise a large stone, which may be dropped and shatter it to pieces at any moment. The figures standing on either side of the shield as supporters, are said to be those of Holbein and his wife, and the head of the man bears certainly a strong resemblance to the artist's undoubted portraits. This device in some of the later editions is occasionally placed at the beginning of the work, though evidently designed for the end, as both the scriptural motto and the nature of the design clearly indicate.

Let those who without sin would live,
Heed all this image doth disclose,
And timely counsel it will give,
Whene'er they go to their repose.

Der ritter ir sept vil geschrieben
Das ir noch ritterschaft must treiben
Aryt dem rock vnd seynen knechten
Euch hilft weder schympf noch fechten

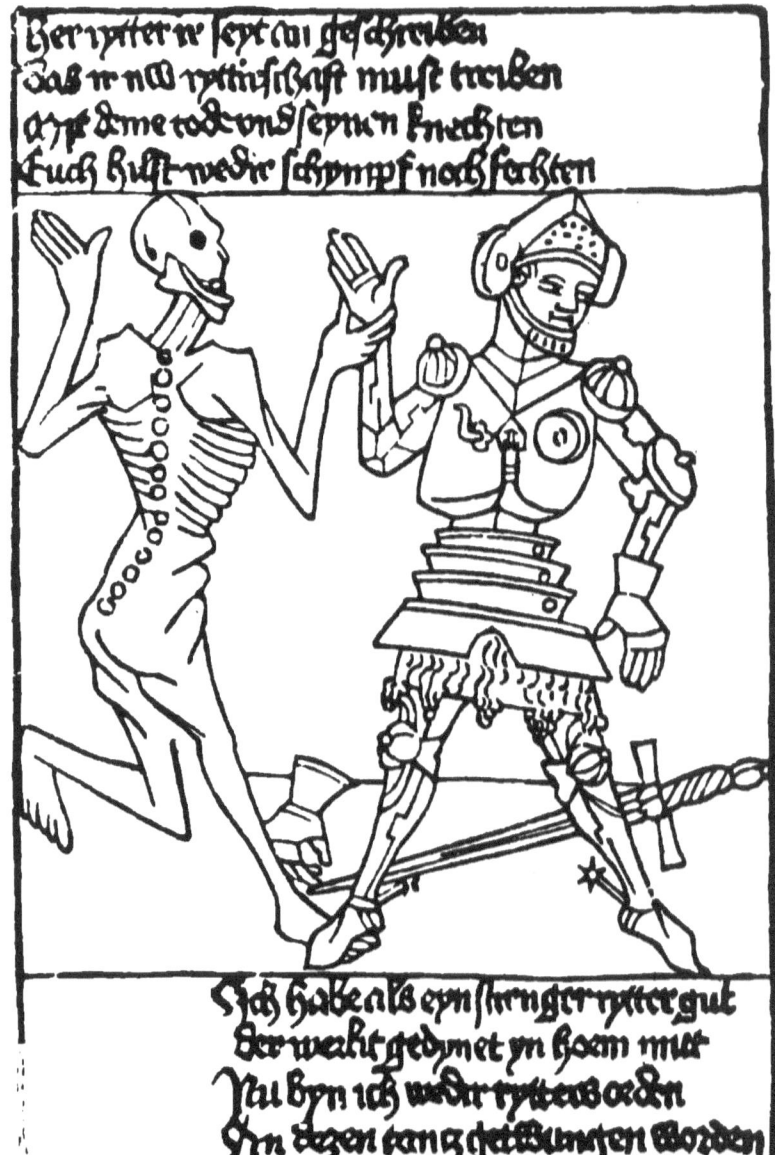

Ich habe als eyn strenger ritter gut
Der welt gedynet yn hoem mut
Nu byn ich weder ritters oedin
In dezen tancz geteübnsten worden

Cur non tollis peccatū meū:ꝗ quare nõ
aufers iniquitatē meã? Ecce nunc iɴ puls
uere dormio:ꝗ si mane me quesieris nõ sub
sistam. ℞. Credo ꝗ redēptor meus viuit
et iɴ nouissimo die de terra surrecturus sū
Et iɴ carne mea videbo deum saluatorē
meū. ѵ. Quē visurus sū egoipse ꝗ nõ alius
ꝗ oculi mei ospecturi sūt Et ĩ carne. Ł.ii.
Edet aīam meã vite mee : dimittã
aduersum me eloquiū meū. Lo-
quar iɴ amaritudine aīe mee. dicã deo. No
li me condēnate. Indica michi:cur me ita
iudices. Nunquid bonū tibi videtur si ca-
lūnieris ꝗ oppꝛimas me opus manuū tua
tum:ꝗ consiliū ipioꝛū adiuues? Nunquid
oculi carnei tibi sunt:aut sicut videt homo
ꝗ tu videbis? Nunquid sicut dies hominis
dies tui ꝗ anni tui sicut humana sunt tem-
poꝛa? Dt queras iniquitatē meã et pecca-
tum meū scruteris. Et scias qꝛ nichil ipiū
fecerim cū sit nemo qui de manu tua pos-
sit eruere. ℞. Qui lazarum resuscitasti a
monumēto fetidū Tu eis dñe dona requiē
ꝗ locū indulgentie. ѵ. Qui vēturus es iu
dicare viuos ꝗ moꝛtuos ꝗ seculū per igne
Tu eis domine dona requiem. ꝗc. ѵ Ł.iii.

THE TREATMENT OF THE DEVICES

OF

THE DANCE OF DEATH,

After the Time of Holbein.

—o—

HERE can be no doubt that the treatment of this series of devices reached its culminating point of excellence under the pencil of Holbein. He enriched the subject with a profusion of imagery, and heightened the sardonic humour with such artistic touches suggested by his prolific fancy, that the subject was at once carried out of the region of the crude grotesque treatment of the earlier phases of mediæval art into a position which placed it upon an equality with the highest class of art of the age. From this high position it gradually declined, though such was the hold which the subject had taken upon the popular mind of all Christianized countries, that ever and anon, at considerable intervals, some fresh artist infused a flash of new genius into the subject, which in the main was dwindling down to weaker and weaker copies (with slight variations) of the devices of Holbein, those of Basle, or those of the oldest French Danses Macabres. It has been shown in the Introduction, that the Holbein treatment of this subject was in many respects distinct from either the "Todten Tantz" of the Germans, or the "Danse Macabre" of the French; differing from both in the number and selection of the subjects, and in the introduction of the features of the Creation and Temptation at the beginning, and of the Last Judgment at the end; as also by the title, which, whether in the Latin or French versions, continued to be of the same import in all the subsequent editions for a considerable period.

The Dances of Death which continued to appear after the time of Holbein may be separated into six distinct divisions. In the first division are those founded on the oldest German printed editions of the "Todten Tantz," of which the Strasburg copy of 1480 (?) is the oldest known example, and of which the subsequent Lubeck editions are perhaps the closest of the later imitations. In the second division are the long series of gradually deteriorating copies of the "Danse Macabre," or French version, which were issued from time to time in Paris, Troyes, and Lyons. In the third division, which is the most numerous, may be classed all the more or less close copies of Holbein's devices, which were published in various parts of Germany and other countries. The fourth division comprises the repro-

ductions in print of the celebrated series of paintings at the cemetery of the
Dominicans at Basle, occasionally mixed with additions from other series.
The fifth division comprises the various modifications, or modernizations,
of one or other of these series ; and the sixth, which is the least numerous,
consists of works exhibiting an entirely original treatment of the Dances of
Death, or closely analogous subjects, with the same or a similar title, some
few of which are of striking merit, but most of them mere vapid and value-
less efforts towards a modern treatment of the great pictorial epic of the
middle ages.   In order to convey a general idea of the character and relative
artistic value of the vast number of editions and variations of the subject
comprised in the above-named six divisions, I have given the following
slight account (in irregular order), of some of the more remarkable of
those which I have had an opportunity of examining.

One of the best of the spurious editions, or piracies, of the Holbein series,
of which the Lyonese publishers complained, appeared at Cologne in 1555,
in which the portrait of Francis I. was exchanged for that of Henry II., the
then reigning king of France ; and a Spanish alphabet of large initial letters,
containing the "Dance of Death," appeared in 1560, also founded on the
devices of Holbein.   M. Vallardi, in his work on the fresco at Clusone,
gives a facsimile from a late German MS. "Dance of Death" evidently
executed at Basle, as it contains a view of that city, but in which the subject
of Death and the Child represented in the facsimile from that MS., is
treated differently from the subject in the Holbein series, or that in the
paintings of the Dominican cemetery : the MS. appears to have been
executed as late as 1560.   In 1590 an imitation of Holbein's cuts appeared
in a pretty little volume published in Venice, the subjects being adorned
with appropriate side ornaments ; and about 1650 appeared a German
edition engraved on copper, with borders composed of sprigs of flowers,
which was the forerunner of many other editions of similar character.   In
1649 the engraver Merian published at Frankfort his copies of the series
painted on the wall of the cemetery of the Dominicans at Basle, which had
just been repaired.   The series, as reproduced by Merian, commences
with the subject of the Preacher, with a congregation consisting of Pope,
Emperor, King, and all other classes, the next subject being the Charnel-
house, and the two figures of Death going forth with drum and fife.   Death
and the Pope follow, in which device Death has a skull swung round his
waist by way of kettledrum, which he beats with a shin-bone,—the Miser
is seized while in the act of weighing his gold as he walks along a country
road,—while the Painter looks round, and sees Death grinding his colours.
The verses being of the same general import as those of the old German
versions.

Hollar's copy of the Holbein series appeared in 1651, with borders
designed by Abraham Diepenbeke.   This series was once much esteemed,
but it is wretchedly inferior to the original devices, though an attempt
was made to heighten Holbein's effects by the addition of stronger contrasts
of light and shade.

In 1654 the original blocks of Holbein's "Dance of Death" appear to have
been still in existence, and were made use of in a Dutch edition entitled
"Doodt vermaskert," and printed at Antwerp, in which eighteen impressions

from the original cuts appear. The retoucher has placed his own name on these blocks, accompanied by the symbol of an engraving-tool, possibly to indicate that he had worked upon them in the way of restoration. A poor imitation of the Holbein devices, with the addition of "The Punishments of Hell," and borders composed of fruit, flowers, and insects, was published by J. B. Mayr, of Salzburg, in 1682.

In 1707, Solomon van Rusting, a physician of Amsterdam, published an entirely new version of the "Dance of Death," with the title "Het Schouwtonnel des Doods," several of the devices of which differ entirely from those of the Holbein, or those of the Basle series, which generally form the basis of such of the late German versions of the subject as are not founded on the devices of Holbein. In the first plate of this work Death places his hand upon Eve while she is in the act of eating the forbidden fruit. Then follows a series, not of single summonses, but wholesale death-scenes; the first being the Destruction of the Cities of the Plain; the second that of the Hosts of Pharaoh in the Dead Sea; while the third exhibits the Slaughter of the Children at Bethlehem, &c. &c.; and in the fourth Death flies, discomfited, as Christ ascends to Heaven. These compositions are followed by some of Holbein's subjects modified; after which several other Dutch versions appeared; among which was the "Kapelle der Dooden," &c., which appeared at Amsterdam in 1750; and a "Toden Tanz" had been published by Imhoff at Basle in 1744, apparently copied from Merian's edition of the devices at the cemetery of the Dominicans in that city.

A very coarse reproduction of the Holbein series, with some additions, appeared in Germany in 1740, while in Paris, about 1770 to 1780, "Girardel Libraire" issued a poor version of the "Dance of Death," without date, under the title of "La Danse des Morts, pour servir de Miroir à la nature humaine, avec le costume dessiné à la moderne." It may be conceived that the wigs, powder, and knee-breeches of the epoch "à la moderne," as boastfully alluded to in the title, do not add either to the impressiveness or the picturesqueness of such a subject.

In 1779 a "Dance of Death," with original devices, was published at Lintz by M. Renz. The plates being large compositions, somewhat in the Boucher style, but with stronger effects of light and shade; the work being, however, without any real artistic merit.

Far different are the claims of a work of similar plan which appeared in 1784, and which is a really clever attempt to treat the subject in a strictly original manner, and in accordance with the spirit of the age, while yet preserving the main import of the more ancient forms of the established versions. This new set of designs was by Schellenberg, who described them as "in Holbein's manner," and the work was published by Heinrich, Steiner, & Co. The style of the artistic treatment is somewhat of the Greuse or Watteau school, which goes well with the nature of the conceptions and the costume and manners of the period. In the first plate, Death is seen as a kind of grim fisherman casting his net over a pair of lovers. In plate 2, a skeleton courtier, in the full court costume of the period, and accompanied by a skeleton lapdog, drops in at the morning toilet of a young girl sitting before her glass, while her pet spaniel, beribboned and rosetted, sniffs very suspiciously at his skeleton relative.

In the next subject, one of the first of the Montgolfier balloon essays
having just taken place, the artist has represented an aërostatic structure
taking fire in the air, and persons throwing themselves from the car at an
enormous height, to escape the flames, while Death sits still, mocking at
the catastrophe, which, with the aid of telescopes, is observed by a crowd
of horrified spectators below.   Death's next travesty is in the form of a
be-plumed and behooped lady of fashion, who jauntily touches a courtier
with the fatal dart in the guise of a fan.   In a nursery scene, Death, as a
nurse, feeds the child in the cradle, while the mother, aware that her child
is taking in death instead of food, wrings her hands in helpless despair.
Other subjects are treated in a similar spirit.   In one, Death presents a
prize in the lottery to an old man, who dies in a paroxysm of joy; in
another, a miser, while counting his gold in a deep chest, is caught guil-
lotine-wise by the falling of the lid, upon which Death leaps in triumph,
squatting upon it with sardonic grin, while gold coins drop from the col-
lapsing hand of the miser.   Then we have Death as the recruiting ser-
geant; and Death, in another device, tumbling a great metal-bound book
on the head of a student, who is reaching it from the shelf.   All this is
original, cleverly executed, and in the spirit of the age.

Bewick's series of copies of the Holbein series appeared in 1789 under
the title of "Emblems of Mortality."   It is a performance quite un-
worthy of the reputation of Bewick, and I should imagine it to have been
the work of prentice hands in his employ, as it does not exhibit one single
stroke of genius in the treatment from beginning to end.   The first piece is
the Triumph of Death, forming a kind of procession, which, after the time
of Holbein, soon became a more or less conspicuous feature in the series.
Mr. Bragg's copy has the autograph of Bewick on the fly-leaf.   Deuchar's
modernized version of Holbein's series was published in London in 1803,
and is wretchedly poor, though it met with considerable success at the
time.   A volume entitled "Death's Doings," by Dagly, with verses by
several contributors, appeared in 1829.   This, also, is a poor production,
and yet the cricket scene, with Death as the bowler, against whose ball
we know that the young batter will not be able to protect his wicket, is
striking in conception, though so poor in execution.

It may be stated here that many recent copies and facsimiles of the
Holbein and other series have been recently published; among which the
one reproducing the Lubeck series is extremely interesting; and at Basle
several editions have been issued of coloured copies of the paintings formerly
at the Dominicans' cemetery.   Of the alphabet, containing Holbein's
"Dance of Death," facsimiles have been published at Munich, Dresden,
and other places.

Among the more recent attempts at an original treatment of the
"Dance of Death," some exhibit artistic merit of the highest kind, more
especially the grandly effective designs of Rethel, whose series of scenes,
founded on the civil convulsions of 1848, and his famous companion
devices, "Death the Friend" and "Death the Enemy," are in some
respects fully equal to the most finely treated of the Holbein devices.   A
recent example, too, almost as striking, appeared in "The Tomahawk," on
the 25th of April of the present year, soon after the fatal accident at the

Bromley Steeple-chase. The example alluded to is a most graphic and spirited sketch, in which a skeleton Death, habited as a jockey, rides by the side of the victim about to take the fatal leap; the device being conceived with a mingling of sardonic humour and tragic earnestness, rivalling even the powers of Holbein or Rethel.

In this brief outline of the direction taken in the artistic treatment of the "Dance of Death" after the time of Holbein, I have not attempted to give a list of all the various editions of different kinds that have issued from the press during more than three centuries and a quarter that have elapsed since the appearance, at Lyons, of Holbein's famous series of devices in 1538. Those who would seek a complete list of all the known editions belonging to that long period, and also to the last twenty years of the fifteenth century, I refer to Brunet and the other well-known bibliographical dictionaries, but more especially to Fiorillo, who, in his "Geschichte der zeichenden Künste," &c., gives a detailed list of more than sixty distinct editions; and also to the works of Massmann and Kestner. Massmann's "Atlas zu dem Werke die Baeler Todtentäntz" (Leipzic, 1847) is most valuable as a book of reference for all the editions of the Basle series, and his "Literatur der Todtentäntz" contains a list embracing editions of the "Dance of Death" of all classes; German, French, &c. M. Kestner, in the "Danses des Morts" (Paris, 1852), gives a still more extensive list, classified in a well-constructed tabular form; and this elaborate work may be consulted with advantage by all who are interested in the origin and successive phases of artistic treatment of the great pictorial epic of the middle ages.

www.ingramcontent.com/pod-product-compliance
Lightning Source LLC
Chambersburg PA
CBHW030610040726
47497CB00008B/2922